A Banquet for
Hungry Ghosts

A Collection of
Deliciously Frightening Tales

A Banquet for
Hungry Ghosts

A Collection of
Deliciously Frightening Tales

Ying Chang Compestine

Illustrated by

Coleman Polhemus

Christy Ottaviano Books

Henry Holt and Company ■ New York

ACKNOWLEDGMENTS

Thanks to my supportive agent, Laura Rennert, who tasted these chilling stories and lived to sell the tales. To my patient husband, Greg, and my smart son, Vinson, my sous-chefs of fright. To my brother Chang Bao and my friend Catherine Cook, whose critiques added zest. A special thanks goes to my talented and beautiful editor, Christy Ottaviano, for going all out to host this banquet. You have all helped cook up this deliciously gruesome feast!

Henry Holt and Company, LLC
Publishers since 1866
175 Fifth Avenue
New York, New York 10010
www.HenryHoltKids.com

Henry Holt® is a registered trademark of Henry Holt and Company, LLC.
Text copyright © 2009 Ying Chang Compestine
Illustrations copyright © 2009 Coleman Polhemus
All rights reserved.
Distributed in Canada by H. B. Fenn and Company Ltd.

Library of Congress Cataloging-in-Publication Data
Compestine, Ying Chang.
A banquet for hungry ghosts / Ying Chang Compestine ;
illustrated by Coleman Polhemus. — 1st ed.
p.   cm.
"Christy Ottaviano Books."
Summary: Presents an eight-course banquet of ghost stories centering
around Chinese cooking and culture. Each story is followed by a recipe
and historical notes.
ISBN 978-0-8050-8208-1
[1. Ghosts—Fiction. 2. Cookery, Chinese—Fiction. 3. Family life—China—Fiction.
4. China—Fiction. 5. Short stories.] I. Polhemus, Coleman, ill. II. Title.
PZ7.C73615Ban 2009   [Fic]—dc22   2008050273

First edition—2009 / Designed by Véronique Lefèvre Sweet
Printed in July 2009 in the United States of America by R.R. Donnelley & Sons
Company, Harrisonburg, Virginia

1 3 5 7 9 10 8 6 4 2

To Vinson Ming Da, my best sous-chef

MENU

Author's Note

While growing up during China's Cultural Revolution, I constantly hungered for food—because it was rationed; and books—because they were burned.

Twenty years after coming to America, I still dream of my beloved hometown, Wuhan, the capital of Hubei province in central China. I dream of shopping in the morning at vegetable markets along the Yangtze River, cooking with my grandmother in our small kitchen, and eating cold noodles in spicy sesame–soy sauce at a street vendor's stall.

I am fascinated with food and strongly believe that it reflects the history and culture of a country. Nearly everything I write has something to do with food: cookbooks and children's books, with a strong emphasis on Chinese cuisine.

Food has always played an important role in Chinese society. Perhaps it is because the country's history of hunger caused by famines, war, and brutal rulers has embedded an obsession about food within its people.

China has a long tradition of honoring the dead with food, stemming from the belief that hungry ghosts linger on to haunt the living. Combining these two important cultural traits allowed me to weave little-known historical details about Chinese history and culture into the ghost stories in this book. More important, it allowed me to continue to sate my appetite—for good food and a good book.

Hungry Ghosts

Hungry ghosts exist in a land of limbo, between the worlds of the living and the dead. They are the spirits of people who often died hungry, prematurely, and unjustly.

According to Chinese tradition, the hungry ghost must be placated with food offerings during the monthlong Hungry Ghost Festival. It starts on the fifteenth day of the seventh lunar month, usually during late August or early September by the Western calendar. This is the time when the gates that keep the ghosts out of the living world open and the dead return to seek revenge and finish unsettled business. They actively seek living souls to replace them in the underworld, especially those who have shown disrespect or have harmed them during their lifetime. For this reason, food is the most important aspect of the Hungry Ghost Festival. When night falls, people place food outside their doors and toss out cookies, dumplings, and other treats into the street. These offerings appease the roaming ghosts and prevent them from haunting their family. However, not all hungry ghosts cooperate. Some still haunt the living, like those in the stories that follow.

The Banquet

An ancient Chinese proverb says, *"Min yi shi weitian*—To people, food is heaven."* Dining plays a central role in all social settings. The most common greeting in China is *"Chi le mei?*—Have you eaten?"*

In the East, it's unthinkable for a person not to share what he orders at a restaurant with his friends or family. The importance of sharing is illustrated by the family style of round-table dining. Various dishes are set on a large lazy Susan for all to enjoy.

A traditional Chinese meal always consists of an even number of dishes to bring good luck and harmony. The word for "eight" in Chinese (pinyin: *bā*)* sounds like the word for "sudden unexpected good fortune" (pinyin: *fā*). So to appease the hungry ghosts, I present this eight-course banquet.

*Pinyin is a method of showing how to pronounce Chinese words using the Roman alphabet.

APPETIZERS

Steamed Dumplings

LONG AGO, IN 200 B.C.E, there was a small village called Bright Stars situated in the northern mountains of China, along the midsection of the Great Wall. The winter was harsh when this section of the wall was constructed. Heavy snowdrifts blocked the narrow paths through the rugged mountains. For months, supply caravans could not make it through to the workforce.

That winter, some of the workers mysteriously vanished. Everyone was puzzled as to where they had gone: There were no roads out, and with no food, the escapees would surely perish in the cold. Desperate to stop the disappearances, the camp master divided the workers into small teams and issued an order to punish the entire unit if one member deserted.

Despite food shortages, workers were forced to labor day and night in two shifts to meet the emperor's demands—one mile of wall per day. Everyone struggled to survive.

However, one inn—the Double Happy—never seemed to run out of food. It served the best steamed dumplings anyone had ever tasted. No one knew how the owner, Mu, a portly and crafty middle-aged man, got the supplies to make his dumplings so delicious.

After the winter storms cut off the caravans, Mu raised his prices daily. Even so, hungry workers waited in long lines outside his inn. Everyone talked enviously about the fortune he was making.

One cold night after the inn had closed, two starving workers broke into the kitchen. They hoped to steal some food before heading to their evening shift. The taller one, with a rope tied around his bulky cotton jacket, tiptoed in behind his friend, whose ragged fur hat covered most of his face.

Full moonlight shone through the tall windows, leaving streaks of illumination on the kitchen floor. In the far corner, white mist hovered above a huge bamboo steamer on the stove. The scrumptious smell aroused their hunger and made them weak. As they reached for the dumplings, they heard scraping and chopping sounds from behind a cabinet next to the stove. They pushed the cabinet away from the wall, revealing a small door. Fur Hat opened it. Instantly, the pungent odors of garlic, ginger, pickled cabbage, meat, and blood repelled them back a step. Mu, the innkeeper, stood silhouetted in the yellow light of an oil lamp. With a cleaver in each hand he hacked at a dark mound of red meat on a heavy rectangular table. Near him, in a pile on the floor, were arms and legs! Most of them had had the meat stripped from their white bones.

When Mu noticed Fur Hat and Cotton Jacket, he waved his cleavers about wildly and ran toward them. Fur Hat was a trained kung-fu fighter. He pushed his friend aside and swept his left leg across the innkeeper's face, knocking him to the ground. The innkeeper's knives whipped narrowly past Fur Hat. The blood from them drew inky red lines on the wooden floor.

The two workers dragged Mu across the room. Cotton Jacket took the rope from his waist and tied the innkeeper's hands to the table's thick legs.

"You watch over him," Fur Hat said as he ran toward the door. "I'll go report this."

"No!" begged the innkeeper. "Please, I'll make you both wealthy. You will never go hungry again."

Fur Hat stopped, glanced at the flesh on the cutting board, and spat at the innkeeper. "How dare you offer me this disgusting meat! I would rather die of hunger—"

"No, no! Of course not! I have roasted chicken, smoked fish, and rice cakes for you." He jerked his chin toward the dark corner. "There, in those jars."

Cotton Jacket reached into one of the jars and took out a chicken wing. He bit into it. Thick brown sauce ran down his large hand. The innkeeper's face lit up. "Well, how about untying me and we'll talk."

Cotton Jacket stopped stuffing his pockets with preserved duck eggs. "How did you kill them?" He tried hard not to look at the bloody pile as he asked.

"Easy!" A grin emerged upon the innkeeper's face. "Like drunk chickens. Whenever I ran out of meat, I offered my last customers some strong sorghum wine. None of them ever refused, and they drank it like water. Once they passed out, I slit their throats. Most of them didn't even wake."

"You devil!" Cotton Jacket ran over and kicked the innkeeper in his side. The innkeeper moaned sharply.

"We can't be late for our shift," said Fur Hat, as he grabbed pieces of salted fish from a jar. "Let's decide what to do with him in the morning."

Ignoring the innkeeper's pleas, they moved the cabinet back into place, locked the door, and headed out into the cold.

That night, a section of the wall collapsed, burying a team of workers alive. Fur Hat and Cotton Jacket were among them.

The next morning, people were puzzled as to why the Double Happy didn't open. Three days later, a group of hungry workers broke in. They ate everything they could find, including the rock-hard, frozen dumplings in the steamer.

Before long, they noticed many large rats with shiny eyes and wiry whiskers, scurrying out from behind the cabinet.

Each carried a strip of dark red meat. The workers moved the cabinet and found the door. Thinking they'd discovered a secret cache of food, they crowded into the room and then quickly fought to get out, shrieking and vomiting as they ran away.

Inside, the innkeeper's trussed body slumped against the table. Scattered near him were the clothes, shoes, and bones of the missing workers.

Large gray rats ran up and down the innkeeper's body, tearing at the remaining tattered organs. Part of his left cheek was missing—and his face was frozen in a primal scream.

That was the last day anyone ever entered the inn, until many years later . . .

In the shadows of the Great Wall stood the ancient brick building once known as the Double Happy. Its large roof floated majestically over its red brick base. The front door opened to the east, facing a long stretch of the Great Wall, winding through the imposing mountains.

Whenever the young people in the village of Bright Stars asked about the building, the elders grew nervous and whispered that the place was haunted. No matter how relentlessly the youths inquired, their elders would say nothing more.

Bright Stars remained a quiet and forgotten place until a successful businessman, Jiang, came to visit his uncle. Tall and skinny, Jiang wore a pair of gold-framed glasses and gleaming black leather shoes—symbols of modern success. His uncle, a small, dried-up man with crooked teeth, proudly introduced Jiang to everyone as his wealthy nephew from Beijing.

He took Jiang to the Great Wall because there was really nothing else worth seeing in this backward village. As they approached the wall, Jiang saw the sinister building standing in the last rays of sunlight.

"Whose house is this?" asked Jiang.

"No one's. It's haunted," said Uncle.

"Haunted?" Jiang laughed dismissively and marched up to the building.

"Don't get too close." Reluctantly, Uncle followed, for he didn't want to upset his rich city nephew.

"Look at its solid condition!" Jiang stroked the brick wall in awe. "You don't see thick walls like these anymore. Slap on some fresh paint, replace a few broken shingles, a couple of warped floorboards, and I could convert this relic into an authentic inn!"

Jiang thought of himself as a smart businessman who wasn't afraid to take risks. After China instituted free-market reforms and allowed private businesses, he'd made a small fortune in real estate and restaurants.

Uncle desperately tried to persuade Jiang that opening a business in Beijing would be much more profitable. No one would be interested in coming to this out-of-the-way place.

But Jiang had set his mind on making a profit off this old haunted house.

Even though Jiang offered high wages, the biggest problem was finding laborers willing to work on his project. A few young villagers were tempted. But when the elders heard them discussing it, they glowered.

"Unspeakable things were done in that house. Don't be part of it. That young man is going to pay for his stupidity."

At last, Jiang had to resort to calling his office in Beijing and having them send out a crew of laborers. Repairing the inn proved to be more difficult than expected. The roof and windows had to be replaced. Furniture had to be bought and rooms redecorated. Each day, while the laborers worked, villagers young and old gathered outside and watched. Two months later, the new inn was ready for business. Jiang placed an ad in an English-Chinese tourism magazine in Beijing:

LOOKING FOR ADVENTURE? COME STAY IN AN OLD HAUNTED INN NEXT TO THE GREAT WALL. EQUIPPED WITH MODERN COMFORTS WHILE RETAINING ITS ORIGINAL CHARM. 50% DISCOUNT FOR THE FIRST TEN BOOKINGS.

When the magazine hit the stands, Jiang's office received a few inquiries, but only one booking—from an American named Dave. Dave was a college student who had come to Beijing to improve his language skills and was hoping to see some of the authentic old China. He was excited to stay at a haunted inn and looked forward to having an adventure that he could boast about to his friends back in the States.

After a ten-hour ride along bumpy, narrow mountain roads, the bus dropped Dave off at a dirt path. He was greeted by a group of villagers who had heard about his arrival. No foreigner had ever come to Bright Stars before, so the villagers were fascinated by Dave's blond hair and found his six-foot height astonishing. A few brave children timidly accepted the sticks of gum Dave offered them. They led him to the inn.

Once there, Jiang warmly greeted his first visitor and apologized for his driver missing him at the bus stop. He treated Dave to his best room on the first floor, next to his.

The chef that Jiang had hired from Beijing had not yet arrived, so Jiang took Dave to his uncle's house for dinner. Uncle lived in a one-story mud house divided into two rooms.

Uncle greeted them warmly at his door. Giggling children with dirty faces crowded behind a big maple tree nearby until Jiang shooed them away.

It took Dave a while to adjust to the acrid stench of sweat and unfiltered pipe tobacco. However, he was delighted to visit a local's home and practice his Chinese. The wooden furniture was rough and stark. Along the far wall was a typical northern farmer's *kang*, built from mud bricks with a stove burning underneath. It served as a bench during the day and as a bed at night. A short-legged table piled high with food occupied the center of the spacious kang. On it were lion's head meatballs, sweet-and-sour ribs, egg foo yung, meat dumplings, and other dishes—many that Dave had never seen before.

Jiang's uncle had spent days preparing an eight-course meal for this special occasion. A round earthen pot rested on the big brick stove that sat in the middle of his living room. Escaping steam rattled the pot's lid. It smelled meaty.

Throughout the meal, Jiang and his uncle kept stuffing food into Dave's bowl. By the end of the meal Dave thought he would explode like a firecracker. Still, acting as a good Chinese host, Jiang's uncle insisted Dave take a bowl of dumplings with him for breakfast.

Back at the inn, Dave said good night to Jiang and retired to his room. He set the bowl of dumplings on a small table near the door, and went to sleep.

A rhythmic knocking awakened him in the middle of the night. Full moonlight shone through the tall windows, leaving streaks of illumination on the floor. Bleary-eyed, Dave stumbled out of bed, accidentally tipping over the bowl. Cursing under his breath, he was picking up the food when he heard scraping and chopping sounds.

Curious and slightly miffed at being awakened, he followed the noises down the dimly lit hall to the kitchen. The rhythmic knocking grew louder. Dave gently pushed against the thick door; it opened slightly.

In the moonlight a horrid, decrepit creature was chopping up chunks of dark red meat with two cleavers. It looked up and spotted Dave.

Whipping its cleavers about, it gave a piercing scream and charged at Dave, who tore away from the kitchen, down the hall, and into his room. Dave slammed the door shut and jumped into bed, huddling against the wall.

Wham! Bang! The cleavers shattered the door into splinters. The creature crashed inside, growling menacingly.

Dave shook uncontrollably as the creature loomed closer, filling the room with the horrible stench of rotting meat. The creature raised its knives and Dave squeezed his eyes shut.

Then came a delighted cry and the knives clattered to the floor. Dave forced himself to look. The creature crouched over the spilled dumplings, hungrily devouring them.

Gathering his strength, Dave jumped through the window and dashed down the dirt path to the village, hollering wildly.

Hearing Dave's cries, the villagers stumbled out of their homes and watched in silence, the elders glancing knowingly at one another. Dave slowed to a halt when he was confronted by Jiang's uncle. Between gasps he told Uncle in broken Chinese what had happened at the inn.

No matter how persistently Uncle begged the villagers, no one was willing to go check on Jiang in the dark. Dave spent the remainder of the restless night at Uncle's house.

At daybreak, the villagers gathered in the street. They brought sticks, shovels, cleavers—any sharp or blunt objects they could find. Dave and Uncle led the way, shuffling nervously toward the inn. Uncle wielded a long machete.

The front door of the inn stood closed. Uncle called out loudly. No answer. Everyone joined in, their shouts echoing from the tall mountains surrounding the village.

At last the door flew open. Jiang appeared in his silk robe, looking confused.

"What's happening?" he asked as he rubbed his eyes.

"Did you hear my screams last night?" asked Dave.

"What screams?" Jiang walked out of the inn. "I have lived in the city my whole life. The noise there is louder than any scream you could dream up."

Uncle shook his head and said, "You shouldn't have opened this inn."

Dave quickly told Jiang what had happened.

Jiang led the group inside. They couldn't find any sign of the ghost, the dark red meat, or the cleavers. If not for the shattered door to Dave's room, Jiang would have thought Dave made up the whole story.

Jiang muttered, "I can't afford to let this great business opportunity be ruined by a ragged ghost. If the dumplings stopped him last night, I will leave more out tonight. Maybe that's all he wants."

The villagers whispered uncertainly.

Jiang straightened his robe and stepped onto the wooden

chair near the front door. "Go home, everyone!" He waved his arms. "Make dumplings. I will pay a good price for them." He turned to Dave and said, "If you stay I will offer you free room and board."

Dave thought for a moment and nodded. He was scared, but what a story he would have to tell back home!

At sunset, Jiang stood at the door, holding a stack of money. Next to him were two big baskets. Villagers arrived in small groups, carrying dumplings in bowls, steamers, and baskets. Jiang handed out money like free movie tickets. It took no time for him to fill his two big baskets. All the villagers were thrilled by the generous pay—except for a group of older people who stood at a distance, whispering darkly among themselves.

Dave helped Jiang spread hundreds of dumplings, surrounding the outside of the inn. Then they locked the doors and windows.

The first part of the evening, they stayed in the kitchen. Jiang turned on all the lights and paced around the room. Dave was the only one who ate the beef noodles and drank the green tea that Uncle had brought for them. "Soon, my chef will be here," said Jiang, deep in thought. "He can make the dumplings, and I won't have to buy them from the villagers."

Dave ignored Jiang and peeked through the curtain. Clouds drifted slowly across the full moon. At midnight, exhausted, Dave went to his room and lay in bed, listening attentively. Fall wind rustled aspen leaves across the ground; apple tree branches gently tapped against the windows. Soon he drifted off to sleep.

Dave was awakened in the early morning by Jiang's yelling, "The dumplings are gone! It worked! It worked!"

The news spread across the village. By lunchtime, villagers were lined up with dumplings to sell. After filling his two baskets, Jiang had to turn away the rest.

The second night, Dave and Jiang, cameras in hand, peeked through the curtains, waiting for the ghost. But it was a cloudy night and too dark to see anything. Worn out, they dozed off, slumped around the kitchen table. When they awoke, the morning sun shone on the front porch.

Jiang and Dave ran outside. "It worked again!" Jiang jumped up and down like a child. "That's all the ghost wants! Dumplings!" Jiang pulled out his cell phone and called the Beijing tourism magazine. The following day, a big ad appeared.

A TERRIFYING GHOST HAS BEEN SIGHTED
AT THE ALL-NEW HAUNTED INN!
AN AMERICAN BOY HAS PROVEN IT TO
BE SAFE! COME JOIN THE EXCITEMENT!

Under the ad was a picture of Dave smiling, holding a big bowl of dumplings. Calls poured into Jiang's Beijing office.

Jiang's chef arrived with the first busload of guests. In the following days, more busloads of tourists came, with or without reservations. The inn was overflowing with well-dressed, loud city tourists. Some were so desperate to stay they told Jiang that they would happily sleep on the floor.

Now acting as a guide, Dave led the tourists to the kitchen and showed them where the ghost had stood. In the last few days, his Chinese had improved so much that Dave regretted he hadn't come to China sooner. He spoke proudly about how the ghost had chased him to his room, and how he had cleverly distracted it with dumplings so he could escape through the window. Everyone praised his pronunciation and vocabulary, but most of all his bravery.

Jiang couldn't stop smiling. He figured that, at this rate, he would not only recover his costs but also have enough money to retire soon.

Jiang's chef was so busy preparing hundreds of dumplings for the ghost that the rich city tourists had to buy food from the villagers—eating everything they were offered.

One grizzled old woman in town ran out of vegetables and, in desperation, served a young couple a plate full of stir-fried weeds from her garden. The couple couldn't stop praising the dish. Soon, other locals started to serve their guests wild mushrooms, weeds, and even bean paste that had been meant for their pigs. They were thrilled to make some easy money.

But at the inn, Jiang wasn't happy with his chef. "I hired you to cook for my guests, too. I can't make a sufficient profit if they don't buy their meals here."

The chef, a short man with a big belly, was chopping meat on the kitchen counter. "I haven't stopped working since I arrived. It takes me hours just to make the meat filling. How can I find time to cook for your guests?"

Jiang thought for a moment and said, "The ghost just wants dumplings. Stuff them with whatever is quick and cheap."

"You are the boss," grumbled the chef. "I will see what I can do."

The next day, after sunset, the chef dragged out a big basket full of dumplings. Excitement grew among the tourists. Jiang stood on the front porch, watching the city folks compete to place the dumplings around the inn. The laughter and delighted shrieks could be heard all across the village.

Around midnight, Dave led his last tour through the kitchen. Then he went to Uncle's house to sleep, leaving Jiang behind with a dozen noisy guests. Teenage boys now filled up Dave's old room. Their loud rock music kept the villagers awake until dawn.

The following morning, snowflakes drifted down. In spite of a poor night's sleep, the villagers gathered outside the inn with rice porridge, hot-and-sour soup, scallion pancakes, and dumplings. They hoped to make another small fortune selling breakfast to the city folks.

No one came out.

At first the waiting villagers dismissed this, saying that lazy city folk liked to sleep late. Lunchtime came and went, and still nobody came out. Tired of standing in the falling snow, the villagers called and yelled. But the front door stayed closed.

Two busloads arrived with new guests. The drivers became grumpy when Uncle told them that the current guests weren't ready to leave.

Dave tried the front door to the inn and found it locked. On his way to the back entrance, he stepped on something hard and round.

He picked it up to examine it but quickly dropped it in fright. "It's a dumpling!" yelled Dave.

The new arrivals rushed over and groped through the snow. They found a few bitten dumplings but the rest were intact.

Worried, Uncle broke in the front door with an axe. When it flew open, the delicious aroma of steamed meat dumplings wafted out into the cold air.

The excited crowd shoved their way through the door, but quickly ran out screaming.

Dave and Uncle entered cautiously.

Inside, bloody limbs lay amid broken cameras. Congealing

blood spattered the white walls. Organs spilled out onto the wooden floor in a slimy mess next to a smashed boombox. Jiang's gold-framed glasses lay beside the kitchen door.

To this day, no one knows what really happened. Legend has it that the ghost didn't like dumplings filled with mushrooms, weeds, and bean paste—so he made his own.

THE GREAT WALL OF CHINA AND CHINESE GHOSTS

In ancient times, China was divided into many small kingdoms until the king of the state of Qin, Ying Zheng, conquered them all. He founded the Qin dynasty and declared himself Qin Shi Huangdi—the first emperor of a unified China—and ruled from 221 to 210 B.C.E.

Soon Shi Huangdi's new empire was in great danger. In the north, the swift Mongolian horsemen constantly looted his villages and killed his soldiers. The border was too long for his army to defend.

To stop the northern invaders, Shi Huangdi decided to connect the northern mountain border walls left by previous kingdoms into one Great Wall. He ordered millions of workers to extend and fortify the wall until it wound through the mountains for more than ten thousand li (or more than three thousand miles—farther than the distance from New York City to San Francisco). That is why it is also called the Ten Thousand Li Great Wall.

Due to the harsh weather, food shortages, and dangerous working conditions, hundreds of thousands died during the construction. There is a saying that the wall was built upon the bones of dead workers.

Eventually, the workers enlarged the old walls to be six horses wide and five men high, with watchtowers placed at intervals along the wall. From them, soldiers could spot the Mongols from miles away. They burned piles of straw and dung to signal oncoming attacks. When the enemy drew near, Shi Huangdi's army lit bales of hay soaked with oil and rolled them down the mountains. They threw large rocks and poured hot oil upon the invaders. Because of the wall, the emperor easily defended his northern border with only a small army.

The Qin dynasty ended soon after Shi Huangdi's death, but the Great Wall, still standing today, remains one of the largest man-made objects in existence.

Westerners often presume that ghosts stay inside "haunted houses" while the Chinese believe ghosts wander outdoors. So leaving food outside the house, as in this story, prevents hungry ghosts from entering in search of something—or someone—to eat.

Steamed Shrimp Dumplings with Green Tea Sauce

To avoid coating the steamer basket with oil, and to keep the dumplings from sticking, place each dumpling on its own thin disk cut from a large, round carrot. When the dumplings come out of the steamer, each has its own small serving tray. As a bonus, you get to enjoy the sweet and tender carrots. For meat dumplings, you can substitute the shrimp with the same amount of ground beef or pork.

Makes 30 dumplings.

Ginger-Garlic Green Tea Sauce

1 teaspoon olive oil or other cooking oil

2 teaspoons loose green tea

1 tablespoon ginger, minced

2 cloves garlic, minced

1 small red chili pepper, minced (optional)

½ cup soy sauce

2 tablespoons lemon juice

2 tablespoons rice vinegar

½ tablespoon sesame oil

Filling

3/4 pound large shrimp

1 tablespoon fresh ginger, peeled and minced

5 scallions, minced

2 tablespoons soy sauce

½ tablespoon rice or white wine vinegar

¼ teaspoon pepper

½ teaspoon salt

2 teaspoons sesame oil

2 large, thick carrots

30 square wonton wrappers

FOR STEAMING

4 green tea bags

▦ In a small saucepan, heat the olive oil. Add the loose green tea and cook, stirring, until the tea is fragrant and crispy, 10 to 20 seconds.

▦ Combine the remaining sauce ingredients in a small bowl. Stir in the green tea and oil. Cover and let the flavors blend in the refrigerator while making the dumplings.

▦ Shell and devein the shrimp. Wash under cold running water. Pat dry with paper towels. Dice into ¼-inch cubes.

▦ Combine the shrimp with the rest of the filling ingredients in a large bowl. Mix well.

▦ Thin-slice the carrots into disks. You'll need one disk for each dumpling.

Set up a space for folding the dumplings. Place a bowl of cold water, the wonton wrappers, the filling, and the steamer basket around your workspace. Cover the wrappers with a moist paper towel to prevent drying. Place the carrot slices in the steamer.

With each wrapper, dip all four edges into the cold water. Holding the wrapper flat on your palm, place about one teaspoon of filling in the center of the wrapper. Bring the four corners of the wrapper up over the filling. Pinch the edges together tightly. Set each dumpling on a carrot slice, leaving a little space between them.

Put hot water in a pot for steaming. Bring the water to a boil. Add the tea bags to the water. Set the steamer on the pot. Make sure the water doesn't reach the dumplings. Steam until the dumpling skins are translucent (10–12 minutes). Serve warm with the sauce.

Tea Eggs

THE SUMMER OF 1975 in Wuhan threatened to be another long and boring season until the horrifying events of that July.

It had been a month since school let out. However, Yun's middle-school principal—a tall, skinny man whose long neck stuck out like a turkey's—had recently opened a fireworks factory in the school. He required all the students to work in the assembly hall every morning and gave each of them a quota of sixty fireworks a day. That first of August was going to be the forty-eighth anniversary of the People's Liberation Army. The principal planned to sell the fireworks to the state-owned shops around town for the celebration.

Whenever someone complained about the heat or the work, the principal stuck out his neck and, in his much-resented gravelly voice, recited his interpretation of his beloved leader Chairman Mao's teachings. His favorite line was "Sweat will purify your revolutionary mind, and work will give you more knowledge than books."

Yun hated the acrid stench of gunpowder and the ugly brown stains it left on her hands, but she was glad to be with her classmates. She could always convince them to play the games she suggested whenever the principal turned the other way. One of her favorites was to challenge her friends to see who could stuff two paper eggs into a cardboard chicken without bursting its stomach open.

Chicken Lays an Egg was one of the fireworks the factory made. When lit, the chicken spun in circles, shooting sparks all around before leaving a little egg on the ground. Yun wasn't sure whether a double-stuffed chicken would lay two eggs or no eggs at all, but the game kept them entertained. More important, she liked being the leader.

The afternoon temperature in the city often exceeded 100 degrees. It was too dangerous to work with explosives in such intense heat, so the principal grudgingly sent the students home at lunchtime. For the rest of the day, Yun had nothing to keep her entertained.

Yun was the only girl of middle-school age who lived in the old brick apartment building located in the hospital compound where her parents worked as doctors. She had befriended the boys who lived there, in a manner of speaking: two seventh-graders like her, Ming and Gui, and one chubby sixth-grader named Bo, whom everyone called Fatso. So far, this arrangement hadn't worked out very well.

One evening in late July as dusk approached, Yun carried out her nightly chores. Like all the other families in the compound, Yun's had no electric fan or air conditioner—so they slept outside in the courtyard. Yun carried a big bucket of cold water downstairs and splashed it under the tall cherry tree. Warm vapor rose into the air as the parched earth instantly absorbed the water. Although her mother insisted that watering made the area cooler, Yun could never tell the difference. She did it only to please her mother.

After pouring out three buckets of water, she helped her father set up two bamboo cots alongside those of the other families. Yun's mother placed dinner on one cot—tea eggs, stir-fried tofu with cabbage, and rice, all bought from the hospital dining hall. The family sat on little stools and ate their dinner, bowls in hand.

"The dining hall's tea eggs are so bland," complained Yun. "And I think the tofu's gone sour." She pushed the piece she had just bitten to the side of her rice bowl.

"Stop being difficult! I've had a long day at work. Besides, it's too hot to cook." Using her chopsticks, Mother deftly placed some cabbage into Yun's bowl.

"Look at your dirty hands. Did you wash them before dinner?" Mother asked in a harsh voice, her eyebrows knitting together in disapproval.

"Dad saw that I did," Yun replied defensively as she

looked at her father for support. He nodded and poured some soy sauce over Yun's tea egg.

"Making fireworks isn't a job fit for children," Father grumbled.

Mother sighed. "You know she has to. Or else she will be expelled from school."

After dinner Yun's father returned to the hospital and Yun cleared away the dirty dishes, her last chore of the day. Her mother gossiped with neighbors while waving a big palm fan. Dragonflies flitted through the dusk to catch mosquitoes.

Yun grew bored of eavesdropping on their rambling conversation about herbal remedies for heat rash. Finally, she couldn't resist the racket the boys were making and went to join them at the far corner of the courtyard, away from the adults.

The boys had drawn a game board on a cracked concrete Ping-Pong table. Ming and Gui were arguing over a game of chess.

"Gui, you cheater!" Ming moved a soy sauce cap.

"Am not! It's my turn!" Gui pushed the cap back.

Bo lay on the ground, shooting marbles, making popping sounds with his mouth each time the glass balls hit one another.

Their faces, painted with streaks of sweat and dust, resembled Chinese opera singers. Their sleeveless T-shirts and shorts were marked with black stripes of grime. Yun warily stood a few meters away, worried that her white shirt would get dirty.

She wished she could think of a game the boys would be willing to play with her, ideally anything where she could stay clean. Like the game they played last summer, where she was the teacher and the boys her students. But to her dismay, this year the boys refused to sit still and pretend to be her students. She watched the chess game with detached interest, trying to come up with something she could convince them to play.

By now the light of a full moon glowed upon the rooftops. Beds, chairs, and tables filled the courtyard, where neighbors sat in groups chatting and laughing as many ate their dinner. A group of old men had gathered around a small table, drinking tea and playing chess under a faint streetlight.

People gradually drifted off to their cots and began bedding down for the night. As the conversations dwindled, someone's snoring punctuated the air, sounding like the street vendor's popcorn machine. The boys' meaningless chess game dragged on. Yun was beginning to think that listening to the adults' gossip wasn't that bad, and was about to return to her cot.

That's when a series of small, distant explosions tore through the air. Colorful fireworks lit the sky. As more went up, they elicited a cheer from the courtyard. Joining the boys, Yun leaned back on the Ping-Pong table and looked up.

"Why are they setting off fireworks today?" asked Yun. "The big celebration isn't for another week!"

"Who cares?" said Gui. "Enjoy the show." A bright flash filled the night sky, followed shortly by a loud boom.

More fireworks shot up, then came a huge explosion—and the cheering faltered. "Something's wrong," muttered a woman nearby. People began to stir among the cots and tables.

A few seconds later, the fireworks ceased. An orange flare lit the sky, and then faded to a steady glow. A siren began wailing, accompanied by frantic screams.

A nurse in a white uniform rushed into the courtyard. "Everyone report to the hospital immediately!" she yelled. "The middle school exploded!"

Panic gripped the courtyard. A few young children started to cry. The adults rushed out of the courtyard in their pajamas, flip-flops slapping their grimy feet. Some still carried their bamboo fans and teacups. Yun and the boys followed them across the street to the hospital.

Injured people arrived in rickshaws, on bicycles, or carried on bamboo beds. One man with a bloody face was missing a hand. Screams of pain filled the street and the air reeked of blood and sweat.

Yun and the boys desperately wanted to know how many people were injured and if their principal was among them. The boys hoped that the explosion had destroyed the factory so they would be free to play all day for the rest of the summer. Yun wondered if the nurse had exaggerated about their school exploding. Surely the sturdy walls would have held together.

They had no way of getting their questions answered. The

adults were busy running in all directions, like ants in a disturbed nest, hardly noticing them. Yun and the boys ducked low and snuck down the street hoping to check out their school. A group of policemen manning a blockade told them to go home. Disappointed, they returned to the empty courtyard and bickered over what to do. At last, they agreed to go to the Room of the Dead, a one-story shed where the hospital kept the deceased. It stood behind the emergency room.

The Room of the Dead occupied the right half of the wooden shed. Two undertakers lived in the other half. One was a tall, skinny man known as Miàn Tiáo—Noodle. The other was a short and fat man whom everyone called Dōng Guā—Melon. They kept their door open all summer, probably because their room had no windows.

However, the Room of the Dead's door stayed shut year round. It had one small window, high up on the wall, on the side opposite the undertakers' door. The window overlooked an open field littered with old furniture and trash.

The group huddled below it. They could hear Noodle and Melon talking, coughing, and moving in and out. What seemed like hours later, all became quiet and the light in the undertakers' room went out.

At first Yun made the boys let her stand on their shoulders to peer through the window, but she kept falling off. Then Gui wanted her and Ming to hold him up, but his feet were stinky so Yun refused. And no one wanted to hold up fat little Bo.

Their arguments woke up Noodle and Melon, who came running out of their room in their nightgowns.

"Go home, you brats!" shouted Melon in his husky voice.

"Leave us in peace!" yelled Noodle.

Yun and the boys ran away screaming. They hid among a line of maple trees—only to return in a few minutes. It wasn't long before they grew too noisy and were chased away again. This time the undertakers stalked around the Room of the Dead, staring out into the shadows and cursing them. Exhausted, the group gave up and went back to the courtyard to fall asleep, exhausted.

When they awoke the next morning, most of the adults still had not returned. Yun and the boys walked out into the street where people gathered in front of the hospital. A rumor had it that the accident was the principal's fault. He had been demonstrating the fireworks on the school's playground to his old army buddies, hoping to land a big sale.

People who lived nearby were preparing to sleep outside when they saw the fireworks. They gathered around to watch, enjoying the show, when one of the rockets flew through the window of a classroom used to store the gunpowder. Seconds later a terrible explosion erupted, resulting in many casualties.

With the factory closed and no parents nagging Yun to do her chores, she spent most of the day huddled outside the Room of the Dead with the boys.

A green military truck arrived late in the morning. Noodle and Melon carried four covered bodies out of the Room of the Dead to the truck. One dead person's feet protruded from under the sheet. They were as pale as the boiled eggs Yun had brought along for lunch.

Later that afternoon, Noodle and Melon carried two bodies from the hospital into the Room of the Dead. The first one was wrapped tightly with a sheet, though Yun and the boys could see that the person was very tall. With the second corpse, the undertakers didn't tuck the sheet around, only draped it over. Her long black hair fell over the side of the stretcher, swaying like strands of seaweed.

"Look at her hand!" Yun whispered nervously.

A dark purple hand dangled alongside the hair, bobbing a little as if beckoning someone to follow. Two fingers were missing.

Ming and Gui ran in fright to hide behind a tree. Bo grabbed Yun's shirt. Despite the growing urge to throw up, Yun didn't move. She wanted to prove to the boys that she wasn't afraid.

Afterward, they argued over whether the tall body was the principal.

When the last glimmer of sunlight slipped below the trees, Yun stood up. "I'm going home for dinner," she announced, disappointed that none of the boys had acknowledged her courage in facing the corpse.

"Ahh, you're just afraid to stay after dark," crowed Gui, laughing heartily, displaying a mouth full of fillings. The other two snickered. Yun took a deep breath and swallowed the angry words bubbling in her throat.

"I am not!" she retorted. "I will return after dinner. And I will stay here longer than any of you, no matter what happens!"

"Oooh! The principal might get you!" said Bo, wiggling his fingers and shaking his head in a way he imagined to be scary.

Yun slapped Bo's hands. "Stop acting stupid!"

The boys chortled scornfully.

"Fine!" said Yun. "I'll meet you here at midnight. If I stay longer than all of you, then I'm the Dragon Head, and you must play the games I like for the rest of the summer!"

"Deal sealed!" yelled Bo. The boys slapped their hands together with a loud smack.

Back in the courtyard, Yun found many people already asleep. She was too excited to finish the meal set out for her. As she lay on the cot next to her mother, she looked at the bright stars and thought, *It will be so nice to be the Dragon Head and have the boys follow me around.*

When the moon peeked over the buildings that surrounded the courtyard, Yun tiptoed away from the cot. She carried her plastic slippers for fear of making any noise and waking her mother.

The three boys were already waiting below the window of the Room of the Dead when she arrived. The full moon hung just above the maple trees across the field, like a round rice cake. The stench of rotting trash filled the still, humid air. Yun's white T-shirt and below-the-knees blue skirt were soaked with sweat.

Following Yun's suggestion, they dragged an old iron bed from the nearby field and shoved it under the window. Then they placed a chair with a cracked seat on it. Everyone crowded onto the bed, elbowing one another for their turn to climb up on the chair and look.

"It's Yun's idea. Let her be the first," said Ming.

Yun gave Ming her most sincere smile and clambered up the tottering chair. Bo squeezed on beside her. She reluctantly let him come up, though the chair wobbled threateningly.

"What do you see?" whispered Gui.

"The light is off. Candles are lit around the room," Bo said in a low voice.

With the light from the moon and the candles, Yun could see the room clearly. One body lay on each of four stone slabs, tucked tightly beneath a sheet. To keep the bodies from rotting in such hot weather, the caretakers had placed big blocks of ice around the slabs. The bodies would be kept there until the families came to take them home for the burial ceremony.

"Two of the bodies are tall. Either one could be the principal," said Yun. "People have sent food."

The staff often sent food and wine for the dead that had no family, to prevent them from becoming hungry ghosts and haunting the hospital. Two bottles of sorghum wine, a basket full of tea eggs, and bowls of food lay on a table against the wall opposite the window. Tea eggs were popular because they were easy to prepare and stayed unspoiled in hot weather.

The strong scents of antiseptics and rotting flesh assaulted Yun's nose. She tried hard not to sneeze, afraid of waking Noodle and Melon.

Gui grew impatient and tried to climb up alongside Yun and Bo. The chair trembled.

"Wait for your turn," Bo protested nervously.

"Let me see!" hissed Gui.

"Shh!" Yun put her finger to her lips. She and Bo got off to make room for Gui and Ming. To Yun's relief, despite all the noise they had made, Noodle and Melon didn't come out to chase them away.

"Black feet are sticking out of one sheet." Gui's voice quavered.

"I think the nearest body is moving!" Ming's voice rose sharply.

A strange choking sound came from inside the room. "K-k-k-kch-kah! K-k-k-k-ah!"

"What's that?" Bo shivered.

"The body is choking." Ming's voice cracked.

"Gach-k-k-k! Kha-k-k-k!"

A chill ran down Yun's spine.

"*Ai yo!* The ghosts are choking!" Gui screamed.

The bed bounced around, nearly throwing Yun up in the

air. She quickly grabbed the back of the chair and crouched down, feeling the strength drain from her body.

"AAAAHHHH! OOOOOH!" The choking turned to long, piercing screams from two different voices.

Goosebumps spread over Yun's sweaty arms.

When the screams stopped, Yun looked around. Gui had run through the open field. Ming and Bo cowered together on the bed near her.

Still wanting to prove to the boys that she was the bravest, Yun took a few deep breaths and gathered up her strength. Gripping the back of the chair, she climbed up and peeked inside.

What she saw made her fall right off, landing on something soft.

"Ouch! Get off me," Bo whined.

"What happened? What did you see?" Ming whispered.

"One . . . one got up . . ."

In a blink, Bo scrambled out from under Yun and ran.

"I—I won't mind playing your teacher-and-student game," Ming said faintly. "I'm going home."

"Please stay with me, Ming! We can take turns being the Dragon Head," Yun begged.

"No, I need to go. I think my mom is looking for me." Ming slid off the bed, backed away from Yun, wheeled around, and ran.

No more noise came from the Room of the Dead.

Still slumped on the bed, Yun tried to stand, but her

knees wobbled like cooked noodles. She scrunched herself into a ball and gasped for air. An eerie silence hung over her as Yun prayed that Ming, Bo—or even that dreadful Gui—would return.

The moon slowly crawled behind thick clouds, and darkness enveloped her. The singing of cicadas and other insects intensified. Only a faint light glowed from the Room of the Dead. Yun's stomach churned with fright. She regretted not running away with the boys.

Stretching her arms across the chair, she tried to pull herself up, but her legs refused to support her. Yun wished she'd never come up with this silly idea.

"Oh-h, I need to get off this hard slab," groaned a familiar husky voice. It was Melon!

"Do you think we scared those brats?" The sound of a cork popping out of a wine bottle accompanied Noodle's raspy voice.

"Of course! Did you hear them scream?" Noodle laughed heartily. "Taste this wine. The dead principal gets better stuff than we do."

It had been a trick!

Yun let out a sigh of relief. She couldn't wait to tell the boys. *The principal did die! I will be the Dragon Head!*

"Here, have a tea egg," said Noodle. "Much more flavorful than the ones sold in the dining hall."

"Well, his lack of a family is our good fortune!" Melon laughed raucously. "I tell you, I have never seen anyone burned as badly as he was, and I have been doing this job since before the Cultural Revolution."

The sounds of dishes clattering, glasses clinking, and lips smacking could be heard out the window.

"Why do you think people sent so much food?" said Noodle. "They must feel sorry for the stupid guy."

Now that Yun knew there were no ghosts, her stomach stopped its frightened churning and growled hungrily. She slid off the chair, scooting to the edge of the bed, ready to go home.

"How dare you drink my wine and eat my food!"

Yun froze. It was a man's gravelly voice, sounding deep and distant, yet vaguely familiar. The sound of eating and of dishes clattering stopped.

"Don't you have any respect for the dead?" the voice shouted.

Suddenly, a terrible clamor erupted. Dishes shattered, and a wine bottle went through the window, barely missing Yun's ear. Wild, piercing laughter clashed with Melon's and Noodle's earsplitting screams.

"I'm going to invite my ancestors for a hot, fresh meal!" The gravelly voice crackled like damp firecrackers.

The moon spun as Yun madly dashed home.

The next day, everyone at the hospital talked about the disappearance of Melon, Noodle, and the body of the principal.

Some said Melon and Noodle had been selling bodies on

the black market, and ran away when they were about to get caught. Others assumed even worse things, yet no one ever imagined anything as terrible as what had really happened—after enjoying a satisfying meal with his ancestors, the principal departed with them.

The city officials permanently closed the school fireworks factory. The boys respected Yun as a real Dragon Head—and she never again led them near the Room of the Dead.

Food Offerings, Tea Eggs, and School Factories

The Chinese use food to celebrate the living as well as honoring the dead. Red banquets are held for weddings and births, while white banquets are held to honor the deceased. After a person dies, the corpse is sent to the morgue, where it waits for the family to take it home for a white banquet. To pay their last respects and ensure the dead won't become a hungry ghost, family and friends bring food in addition to flowers. For the dead that have no family, people send food to the morgue to ensure that they will not come back to haunt the living as angry, hungry ghosts.

Eggs symbolize peace and happiness. Tea eggs are a popular choice to serve to the dead for their journey to the underworld. Tea and spices help keep eggs fresh for days without refrigeration, and boiled eggs are easy to transport.

I grew up in a hospital compound where my parents were doctors. The hospital's Room of the Dead was a constant source of fascination for me and my friends. Many mysterious events happened around the Room of the Dead. It became local news when one of the undertakers died suddenly. The cause of his death was never clear.

During the Cultural Revolution (1966–1976), the Chinese leader Chairman Mao ordered the young people to learn from the working class. To follow his teaching, many schools had factories on site. Students had to work in the factories through-out the school year, and during breaks. Occasionally, accidents occurred due to poor equipment and lack of regulations.

When explosions at fireworks factories garnered inter-national headlines, the government shut many of them down.

TEA EGGS

In China, this is the best-known dish cooked with tea. The tea's flavor and color seep through the cracked shells into the eggs. The longer the eggs soak in the sauce, the more flavorful they become.

Makes 8 Tea Eggs.

8 eggs

5 black tea bags

1½ inch cinnamon stick

½ teaspoon five-spice powder

3 whole dry chili peppers (optional)

5 thin slices fresh ginger

½ cup soy sauce

▦ Place all ingredients in a large saucepan. Add just enough water to cover the eggs and bring to a boil over high heat. Reduce heat to medium-low and cook 15 minutes.

▦ Remove the eggs. With the back of a large spoon, lightly tap the eggs over the entire shell to produce a spiderweb of cracks. Do not peel. Return the eggs to the sauce.

▦ Reduce heat to low. Cover and simmer for 30 minutes. Let the eggs stay in the sauce until time to serve them.

▦ Peel the eggs and remove any membrane. Serve sliced, quartered, or whole at room temperature.

MAIN COURSES

Beef Stew

CHOU WASN'T A BAD MAN. In fact, he wasn't even stupid or lazy. True, he had a few minor flaws. Occasionally he lost his temper, and perhaps he was a bit too passionate about gambling at the mahjong table.

Aside from playing mahjong, he lived a dull life similar to those of the many young men in China who had failed the university entrance exam.

Chou had certainly given that all-important exam his best effort. After struggling through three grueling years of high school and another year of college-prep classes, he had missed the required entrance score by only five points. If his parents had been wealthy or well connected, he would have gained admission to a third-rate university.

Those five fateful points dictated what became of his life.

Instead of getting into a university and eventually landing a comfortable government job, Chou was reduced to laboring at a small neighborhood butcher shop.

The store was located in the corner of an old single-story stone building surrounded by glistening new high-rises. During the two years that Chou worked there, new construction projects shot up like bamboo after the spring rains.

Chou had decided to take this job because he expected to get a discount on ingredients for his favorite dish—beef stew.

It didn't turn out that way.

His boss, a pudgy woman with a garlic-clove–shaped nose, had sharp eyes. Not only did she refuse Chou the slightest discount, he wasn't able to swipe even a scrap of meat. The one time he tried to put a piece of beef into his backpack, he was caught and docked half a week's pay.

To save money, his stingy boss removed all but two of the bare lightbulbs in the shop. Even on the sunniest days, the shop was cast in a gloom of deep shadows. This caused Chou to frequently trip over buckets and water hoses, and more than once he cut himself while butchering an animal. Chou felt resentful toward the world and thought himself much smarter than his four middle-aged female co-workers. They were illiterate, twittering, mindless gossips. His boss was a perfect example. Once her large mouth opened, the words flowed without end. Chou's spiteful nickname for her was Broken Faucet. He hated her ridiculous demands and expectations.

One evening while playing mahjong, Chou won a new, lime green iPod from a fat kid who was constantly picking his nose. His father worked for one of those wealthy joint-venture companies.

Chou could never have afforded an iPod with his miserly paychecks. It became his most precious possession. After someone told him that he had the same high forehead and square jaw as the famous rock singer Shiong Du, Chou downloaded all the bootlegged copies of Shiong Du's songs he could find on the Internet and listened to them constantly. It helped him to cope with the monotony and drown out his co-workers' relentless chattering.

While he enjoyed the music pounding in his ears, he also tuned out too much of what was going on around him. Customers often complained when he gave them beef intestines instead of pork blood, or one pound of chickens' feet when they had ordered pigs' tails.

One day, an old lady offered Chou advice. "Turn down your music, young man, or you are going to be deaf like me!"

Chou rolled his eyes and slapped her order—half of a pig's head—on the counter. The old lady grabbed it and hobbled out in a huff, muttering under her breath about the younger generation.

Chou's bad manners enraged Broken Faucet. "Treat elders and customers with respect!" she yelled at Chou even before the old lady had walked out the door.

For the rest of the day, she hounded Chou endlessly

about everything from his bad attitude to his long hair and baggy pants. Chou did his best to tune her out as he angrily chopped the other half of the pig's head into small pieces.

Although Chou hated his boss, he never thought of killing her.

It happened on a Wednesday morning. Chou was late for work again. It had already been a hard week for him at the mahjong table. Hoping his luck would take a turn for the better, he'd bet more and more money with each round. In the end he lost his whole month's salary and got into a fight that left the right side of his face in staggering pain. He trudged into work hungry, tired, and in a terrible mood.

As Broken Faucet berated him for being late and lazy, Chou turned up his iPod and walked to his workstation, which was piled high with plucked chickens. He picked up a sharp cleaver and skillfully sliced off chicken wings. Every day he had to dissect hundreds of birds. The breasts and legs went to the new restaurants spaced among the high-rises; the neighborhood's old women bought the wings, organs, heads, and feet by the pound to make stew or soup.

Broken Faucet walked closer to Chou as he tossed a handful of chicken entrails into a bucket. Bloody water splashed onto her rolled-up pants. Her eyes narrowed into slits, glowing with anger. Her garlic nose twitched. "I have had it with you! Give me that!" She snatched the iPod out of Chou's pocket, ripping the earphones from his ears.

"Hey! Give it back!" Chou turned to grab it.

"Go get it!" With a malicious grin, Broken Faucet threw the iPod into a bucket full of animal guts.

Chou's face turned white. He stared in disbelief as his iPod sank among the intestines and the headphones floated to the surface of the bloody water. His co-workers giggled.

"You fat pig!" screamed Chou.

"What did you say?"

Broken Faucet slapped Chou across the injured side of his face. When her hand came down the second time, Chou raised his arm to block her blow. As he told everyone later, he had forgotten about the cleaver in his hand. The flat blade cut deep into Broken Faucet's neck.

For a brief moment, no one moved. Faint gurgling replaced Broken Faucet's yelling. Eyes wide, she reached slowly for the cleaver as she toppled backward, knocking over the bucket. Blood burst out of her artery, spraying Chou's hair and face. Broken Faucet twitched on the floor.

The other women ran out of the store, screaming. They shed their bloodstained rubber gloves and dirty slippers on the way out. Chou shook with anger and fear. He fell to his knees and stared in horror at Broken Faucet as her warm blood mingled with the animal viscera. He didn't move until the police arrived to arrest him.

When the police examined Broken Faucet, her throat was so deeply cut that her head hung by a thin flap of skin.

Chou was shocked that Broken Faucet had died so readily, when it was so much harder to slaughter an animal.

He thought about what would happen to him.

If he was lucky, he would only get a few years in prison, like the old man who once lived next door to his parents and had accidentally killed his friend during an argument over a game of chess. If he was unlucky they would sentence him to death. Even then, he thought, it was not the end of the world. After he failed the college exam, he started to believe in Buddhist reincarnation and often daydreamed about his next life being better.

The week before Chou's trial, a woman accompanied by two policemen came to his cell. She had smooth, light skin and deep brown eyes. Her round spectacles and kind smile would have made Chou mistake her for a teacher—if it hadn't been for her deep blue police uniform. She pulled out a stethoscope and some other instruments from a black leather bag and gave Chou a medical checkup, even taking a blood sample.

As she examined Chou, she talked courteously, asking him what he liked to eat.

"Beef stew," answered Chou. Feeling less timid, he added, "Yes, beef stew, especially when it's just a little spicy, and the beef is nice and tender in a thick broth."

She smiled at Chou, who had the trace of a sparkle in his eyes. "You look very calm, considering your circumstances." She straightened Chou's shirt after listening to his heart.

Chou shrugged. "I didn't mean to kill her. It was an accident. Everyone should be able to see that."

"Well, she is dead. And the witnesses do not speak in your favor. You could still receive the death penalty," the officer said in a soft voice.

To show that he was not afraid, Chou said, "As long as I die in one piece, I'll be reborn in twenty years." He turned his head away from her, not wanting her to find any fear in his eyes.

When he looked up again, he saw that she was still smiling. Chou wondered if she thought the notion of reincarnation silly or quaint.

"What kind of music do you like?" she asked as she wrote down the number from the digital thermometer.

"I'm a big fan of Shiong Du." But he was too embarrassed to tell her why. "I really like his new song, 'Trace This Light.'"

"Yes, that is a great song," agreed a male officer, who was packing Chou's blood sample into a plastic bag.

Talking about music reminded Chou of his iPod. If only he hadn't won the iPod, he would have avoided all this misery! His eyes began to mist over.

Glancing up, the female officer seemed to notice how Chou's composure had slipped. She gently placed her hand on his narrow shoulder, looking into his small round eyes. "If you do receive the death penalty, don't worry about the 'final day.' You won't feel a thing."

Chou lowered his eyes to stare at a dirty brown stain on the wall next to his cot.

"How many shots?" he whispered.

She stroked Chou's back and said, "The marksman is well trained. One bullet through your heart is all it takes."

Chou struggled to quell his tears. Her soothing voice reminded him of the kind teacher who had confidently assured him that he would pass the university exam.

After she left, Chou regretted that he hadn't asked what she thought his chances would be. The way she talked worried him.

The day of his trial, Chou waited for hours in the crowded lockup. Finally an officer led him into the courtroom. There he met his defense attorney for the first time, a lanky young man with bad acne. He limply shook Chou's hand and wished him luck.

A bailiff at the front of the room called everyone to attention. "Now begins the case against Wu Chou for the act of murder," he announced. "The honorable judge Li Zen presiding."

Everyone stood. The judge, a corpulent man, sat down on his large black chair, took a sip of his tea, and waved for everyone to be seated. "Evidence against the defendant?" he asked in a lazy tone.

The prosecuting attorney stood up. His gaunt face had an unhealthy yellow cast and his eyes were sickly gray. "The defendant was caught at the scene. His fingerprints were on the murder weapon." He massaged his lower back as he continued. "He does not deny that the unarmed victim died at his hand, by a vicious strike to the neck." He held up a labeled plastic bag that contained the bloodstained cleaver.

Chou stood up, wanting to tell the court that he had forgotten he was holding the cleaver. His attorney dragged him down.

The judge shot Chou a disapproving look. "Witnesses!" he ordered. The prosecutor called on Police Chief Lo to take the stand. From the chief's baggy eyes and bloodshot nose, Chou could tell he was a heavy drinker.

Chief Lo's testimony was brief. "Four witnesses saw the murder. They all said that the attack was unprovoked."

"Unprovoked?" Chou yelled. "She destroyed my iPod! She hit me!"

The judge banged his gavel and ordered Chou to remain silent.

"Defense?" called the judge.

Chou's attorney stood up. "Before this incident, Mr. Wu Chou had a clean record," he said in a timid voice. "As for being unprovoked, the victim destroyed Mr. Wu's property . . ." He paused and looked at his notes. ". . . and physically attacked him. It is true he struck back, but he had no intention to kill her, or even injure her."

The judge fumbled a pill out of a small bottle. "How could he not intend to harm her when attacking her with a cleaver?" he asked scornfully, and popped the pill into his mouth.

The attorney looked at Chou doubtfully, and then in a quavering voice said, "He forgot he was holding it."

The audience in the courtroom gallery tittered. The judge snorted as if suppressing his own laugh, and then rapped the gavel lightly a couple of times.

"Wu Chou, stand to receive your sentence."

Chou felt the room spin. His attorney shook his head sadly and helped Chou up.

"Wu Chou, the court of the People of China pronounces you guilty as charged. You are hereby sentenced to death."

Chou's attorney cried out, "Your honor, I object! The sentence is much too harsh!"

The judge scowled. "The law is clear: a life for a life, no loopholes, no exceptions!" He rapped the gavel, hard. "The execution will be carried out in two weeks. Next case!"

"This is not fair!" cried Chou. He hurled his lawyer's teacup, shattering it against the front of the judge's desk. Several officers jumped on Chou and wrestled him to the ground.

Judge Li rapped his gavel. "Get him out!"

Chou couldn't believe that in less than five minutes, his fate had been decided. He felt angry that he was going to die for Broken Faucet. What would have happened if he hadn't blocked her slap? He fumed at the thought of just letting her hit him.

In some ways, the last two weeks of Chou's life were the best. No one nagged or yelled at him. He had a quiet cell all to himself where he could sleep late, watch TV, and read Japanese graphic novels. If only the food was better—

more meat, fewer pickled vegetables, and fish without the unpleasant odor.

He did miss playing mahjong. Of course, he had nothing to bet, and, even if he won, he couldn't spend the money. But still, playing was half the fun.

His emotions fluctuated. First he fantasized that the court would let him live. It had been an accident, and the authorities would realize that a young man could contribute more to society alive. After the trial, he became angry. Worthless lawyer!

Eventually, he grew weary of being angry. Even though he wasn't very religious, he prayed. "Ancestors, please help me escape death! I promise to treat all elders with respect."

Just as at the mahjong table, he saw no sign that his ancestors were listening. Depressed, he wept into the small hours of the night until exhausted.

The morning of Chou's final day, a mouthwatering meaty aroma awakened him. He inhaled deeply, savoring the scent. After a long yawn, he kicked off his tattered blanket and climbed out of bed. Two guards brought in his last meal and set it on a small table before him. It consisted of a bowl of steaming beef stew, a plate full of deep-fried bread, and a bottle of Tsingtao beer.

His eyes glittered and his thick eyebrows lifted at this pleasant surprise. He sipped the hot broth eagerly, and soon it brought beads of sweat to his high forehead. Chou smacked his lips and moved his mouth like a hungry horse as he chewed the big chunks of tender beef. The stew was well seasoned, with a touch of spiciness, just the way he liked.

One guard set a boombox outside his cell and played "Trace This Light." For a moment, Chou was carried away by the lyrics:

> *This light will lead you through your lonely journey.*
> *Trace this light,*
> *to the end of your life.*

Tears gushed out of his eyes, though he squeezed his lids to force them back. He was so touched and wished he could express his gratitude to the female officer. No one else had ever cared much about what he said.

Despite the fact that his mind kept wandering to his execution, Chou had a strong appetite. Resigned to his fate, it wasn't hard for him to shift his focus back to the delicious food and cold beer in front of him. He had found some comfort in his belief in reincarnation. Surely, in his next life the meat shop would be torn down, and iPods would be even smaller, with batteries that lasted longer.

Chou had hardly finished chewing the last piece of beef when two guards came in, lifted him to his feet, and pulled his arms high behind his back. They skillfully tied them together with thick ropes. The shorter guard plugged his mouth with a dark green cloth and hung a wooden board on a rough cord around his neck. It proclaimed, in bold characters, MURDERER! PENALTY: DEATH.

They led him out of the building and shoved him up a ramp onto the back of a flatbed military truck. Five stone-faced guards crowded in behind him. Chou was disappointed that he was the only prisoner. No one else was there to share the burden of dying.

He knew he would be paraded around the city as they always did with criminals who had been sentenced to death, to set an example to the rest of the populace.

The bright spring sun shone upon his newly shaven head and the gentle wind blew against his face. The scent of fresh magnolia blossoms drifted lazily in the air. Chou was calm, considering the circumstances. He looked around as the truck drove through the city. People lined up on both sides of the street. No one threw rotten eggs at him, like they had at the child abductor. He thought Broken Faucet must not have been too popular.

His mahjong buddies stood in the crowd waving sadly. He would have liked to say good-bye but, with the rag in his mouth, he couldn't move his tongue. His eyes grew moist and his jaw ached.

When he passed the butcher shop, Chou saw his former co-workers talking excitedly. They looked thrilled to see him. Chou viciously glared at them, but they only smiled back. He was disappointed that he didn't see his parents. Maybe they were too angry or ashamed to come. He hoped he would be reborn into a better family that had money and power.

Chou's mood shifted when the truck turned onto a long, narrow road lined with white and pink oleander bushes. The landscape changed from high-rises and crowded shops to utility poles and expanses of rice fields. Despite the cooler, fresher air, his shirt dampened with sweat.

Large bulletin boards swept past. One that appeared frequently showed an attractive woman in an army uniform standing before the Great Wall, holding up a bottle. The slogan declared, ENJOY REFRESHING LONG MARCH COLA!

Chou had seen movies where the victim was shot but lived for a while, writhing in agony. The thought made him shiver. He imagined the worst would be when the bullet hit, ripping into his chest.

Half an hour later, the truck passed through a wooden gate. Above it a sign proclaimed, in large red characters, POLICE SHOOTING RANGE.

Beyond the gate, the truck slowed and came to a stop in an open grassy field surrounded by high wire fences.

Chou suddenly felt nauseated. The gag was soaked with his saliva and tasted greasy, yet his lips were dry and his eyes burned from riding in the wind.

The guards shoved him off the truck and pushed him toward a green jeep parked to the side. To his relieved surprise, the female officer got out. Chou was relieved to see her. With her presence, he felt calmer. He wished they would remove the gag before the final moment, so he would have a chance to thank her for the beef stew and music.

Ignoring his nod of greeting, she pulled out a large syringe from a black leather bag and took hold of Chou's left biceps. He felt the needle puncture his arm through his shirt. He wondered if this was supposed to prevent him from feeling pain.

Instantly, a burning sensation swept through his body. He cried out, but only a muted groan got past the gag. He felt like he was floating. His legs trembled as if made of tofu. Chou would have fallen to the ground if not for the guards supporting him by his arms. His limbs became numb and his mind grew sluggish.

They dragged Chou unceremoniously to a thick oak tree in the center of the field. Crusty stains, the dark brown of dried blood, covered the bark. Chou guessed the little holes and chips in the trunk were from bullets that had passed through other convicts.

As one guard removed the sign from around his neck, the others secured him to the tree. Someone tied a dark scrap of cloth over his eyes. It stank of sweat. Chou felt indignant that they couldn't even give him a clean blindfold. *How many prisoners have died wearing it?*

Footsteps crunched across the field, followed by the crisp snap of a safety clicking off. Chou's breath shortened as he waited for that one shot to his chest. He wondered if his thorax would explode like in the executions in the movies.

Nothing happened.

Then he heard car doors opening and closing. *That must be the hearse to carry away my body.*

A man's deep voice bellowed, "Ready! Fire!"

Chou heard a small muffled explosion. The impact of the bullet snapped his head against the tree. A sharp pain surged through the left side of his chest, but he could still feel his heart beating strong. Blood ran down his sweat-soaked white shirt.

How could he have missed so miserably? It wasn't even near my heart. Chou felt cheated. *The executioner is not well trained at all!*

Footsteps ran toward him. Within seconds, rough hands placed Chou on a stretcher. The blindfold was knocked off his eyes. Guards carried him to a large van full of medical equipment and instruments.

Two men and the female officer stood around him, fully clad in white surgical gowns and gloves. They ripped opened his clothes.

Had they changed their mind about the death sentence? Chou desperately wanted to ask, but he couldn't make any sound past the gag. A couple of flies buzzed eagerly around him.

"Idiots!" yelled the female officer. "They shot his lung!"

"Hurry! He's bleeding badly!" said a slender male officer, lifting up a trash bag. "Hemorrhagic shock could damage the rest of his organs."

The other man picked up a small cooler. With a sharp

scalpel, the female officer skillfully cut deep into Chou's stomach. He gave out one long scream but no one seemed to hear—or care.

The female officer lifted up loops of intestines and dropped them into the trash bag. "Let's get the kidneys first," she said in her soft, commanding voice. "My husband desperately needs one."

Gut-wrenching pain sucked away his breath. His throat tightened. As life drained from his dissected body, he was enraged not by his death, but by the fact that now he could never be reborn. For the first time in his life, he was determined to do *something*. He wanted to destroy and slaughter them all!

A year later, the following anonymous posting appeared on a popular Chinese blog site:

> There's an odd similarity between three men recently charged with murder. All of them received organ transplants last spring. The donor is unknown but is believed to have been an executed criminal.
>
> The first man, a lawyer renowned for his prosecutorial zeal, had his kidneys replaced due to severe damage from kidney stones. After his discharge from the hospital, he ate nothing but beef stew. One day, his wife, the medical examiner for the police department, served him pork stew instead. He became enraged and slit her throat.

The second man, a police chief, received a liver transplant due to his excessive drinking. After being discharged from the hospital, he played "Trace This Light" loudly and continuously. His neighbors went to his door to complain. According to one of the survivors, the police chief withdrew into his room and returned moments later with a cleaver. He sliced their throats, killing two and severely injuring three before being subdued by a blow to the head.

The last man, a grossly overweight judge, had to have his fat-clogged heart replaced. After being discharged from the hospital, he compulsively gambled at the mahjong table. One day, after losing badly, he slashed the other three players' throats with a cleaver.

You won't read about these killers in the obituaries anytime soon. They are all rich and powerful. Without a doubt they will avoid the death penalty, as they have been sent to a comfortable mental hospital.

The following day, the above posting was replaced by a statement from China's Ministry of Health:

When a condemned prisoner insists on donating his organs as an act of redemption for his crime, we should not betray him . . .

UNIVERSITY ENTRANCE EXAM, MAHJONG, AND ORGAN HARVESTING

In 1980, I experienced firsthand the fiercely competitive Chinese university entrance exam, which lasts for three days. That year only one in one hundred students passed. I was among the lucky ones. Recently, my niece and nephew took the exam, and I learned that it's still as challenging.

The future for teens who fail the exam is grim, especially for those that come from families without connections or money. They have few options other than low-paying, often monotonous city jobs.

Mahjong is a popular four-person board game that originated in China. It involves skill, strategy, and reckoning as well as luck. It's most often played with tiles instead of cards. Players shuffle the tiles around at the beginning of the game, and divide them all up. Each player then erects their own "wall" on the table in front of them. Perhaps because such a setup prevents cheating, mahjong has become a popular gambling game.

In the 1950s, the Communist government suppressed mahjong and all other forms of gambling as they were symbols of capitalist corruption. After the Cultural Revolution, mahjong once again became a favored game in China. In 1998, the China State Sports Commission published a new set of laws widely recognized as the Chinese official rules for mahjong. The goal was to change the image of mahjong from a gambling game to a "healthy sport." The new laws stress that mahjong should be a sport and no drinking or smoking is to take place while playing. Today, despite these regulations, the game is widely played in private accompanied by drinking, smoking, and, of course, a great deal of betting.

According to the Chinese government, the organs of executed prisoners may be harvested only if the prisoner or his family consents or if relatives are unwilling to claim the corpse. Recently, the government issued strict regulations against the illegal harvesting and selling of prisoners' organs. Not long ago, authorities announced the arrest of a Japanese man for illegal organ brokerage in China.

BEEF STEW

This dish makes a savory main course for a spring meal; it's filling but not too heavy. It may nurture your kidneys, calm your heart, and strengthen your liver.

Makes 6–8 servings.

> 2 teaspoons all-purpose flour
>
> 1 teaspoon salt
>
> 2 pounds chuck or round steak, cut into 1½-inch cubes
>
> 2 tablespoons extra-virgin olive oil or vegetable oil
>
> 4 garlic cloves, minced
>
> 3 whole red chili peppers, fresh or dried (optional)
>
> 2 teaspoons curry powder
>
> 6 cups beef broth
>
> 1 large purple onion, cut into 2-inch wedges
>
> 4 medium carrots, peeled and cut diagonally into 2-inch-long chunks
>
> ½ pound red potatoes, peeled and cut into 1-inch chunks
>
> 1 large Granny Smith apple, peeled, cored, and cut into 1-inch chunks
>
> Salt to taste

■ Combine flour and salt in a large bowl. Add beef cubes and toss to coat. Heat oil in a large pot or Dutch oven over medium-high heat. Sauté the garlic and chili peppers until fragrant, about 30 seconds. Add the beef and brown on all sides.

■ Add curry powder. Cook and stir for 2 minutes. Add the broth, onion, carrots, and potatoes. Cook and stir for 1 minute. Bring to a boil, then reduce heat to a simmer and cover. Cook for 1 hour.

■ Add apple and cook for 15 minutes more, or until the meat is tender and the broth has thickened. Season with salt. Serve hot.

Tofu with Chili-Garlic Sauce

IT WAS A PERFECT LATE-SUMMER MORNING. A few white clouds decorated the crystal blue sky. Palm trees lined the wide street and a cool breeze, heavy with the scent of salt, flowed through the open top of the bright red BMW convertible. The crisp air reminded Dr. Zhou that the ocean was nearby.

Dr. Zhou was in a very good mood, despite his recent difficult divorce. Today he looked forward to a banquet hosted by the city mayor. Driving through the hospital gate, he waved cheerfully to the two guards before making a left turn. He parked his car on the far side of a six-story building, hoping to avoid patients' families.

From the corner of his eye, Dr. Zhou spotted Mr. and Mrs. Ren. He sighed. The bookish middle-aged couple were working their way toward him through the parking lot. He had met them briefly a couple of days ago, when their son first arrived at the hospital.

Well, he still had a trick to play. As he got out of his car, he pulled his cell phone from his pocket, pressed it to his ear, and talked animatedly to an imaginary listener. Sometimes intellectuals like the Rens were too timid to interrupt a phone call.

"Please excuse us, Dr. Zhou," Mr. Ren said delicately. "May we talk with you?" The man pushed up his black-framed glasses with two fingers.

Annoyed that his little trick didn't work, Dr. Zhou put on his public face and looked up, as if surprised. He recalled that Mr. Ren was a reporter for a small local newspaper, *Ocean News*.

"Yes! Can you wait for me in my office?" He stuffed the cell phone into his black leather briefcase.

"We did, all day yesterday," Mrs. Ren said quietly. "Then we heard that you were arriving this morning to perform surgery on our son. So we decided to try to catch you here."

The two were dressed in the kind of cheap button-down shirts and rubber shoes that vendors sold on the street. Clutching each other's arms, they formed a wall, flanked by the cars on either side.

"W-we had hoped to invite you to a banquet before the surgery," continued Mrs. Ren, the freckles moving slightly on her upturned nose. "But your assistant, Dr. Yan, said you no longer attend them."

"Yes, that's correct." Dr. Zhou patted his belly. "I have to watch my cholesterol. Besides, I'm too busy these days to attend all my patients' banquets."

In truth, Dr. Zhou had stopped accepting invitations to avoid answering endless questions from his patients' families. He was also growing tired of the same dishes served at the sixteen-course banquets: shark's fin soup, shredded lobster in XO sauce, roast duck served with paper-thin pancakes, seasoned crabmeat in coconut shells, fried fish carved into the shape of squirrels, and warm tofu with chili-garlic sauce.

He'd tried them all, or so he thought.

However, today's banquet after the surgery was an exception. The mayor had promised a special delicacy.

Considering all the good food Dr. Zhou had been consuming lately, he was in relatively good shape, thanks to his weekly visits to an exclusive gym. He would have looked a few years younger than forty-five if not for the receding hairline and slight potbelly.

"Now, if you will excuse me . . ." He made a shooing motion.

"The operation . . ." said Mr. Ren, as he reluctantly stepped aside. "Can you assure us that it is safe?"

Dr. Zhou raised his eyebrows. "Did Dr. Yan not describe the procedure to you? He should have given you our brochure as well."

"Yes, he did, but we hoped to discuss it with you," said Mr. Ren firmly.

"Ablative surgery is very straightforward." Dr. Zhou started walking. "I've performed the procedure hundreds of times. No surgery is completely without risk, but complications are rare, and I'm sure if you read the brochure you'd know . . ."

Dr. Zhou increased his pace, but the couple kept up.

"But you're going to drill into our son's head!" Mr. Ren exclaimed.

Annoyed, Dr. Zhou cleared his throat, preparing to deliver a speech he had made many times. "Yes, only three small holes. And this is done with the utmost caution. Then three very thin needles are inserted, to precise depths and locations. The needle tips are heated to exactly ninety degrees Celsius for exactly sixty seconds—enough to destroy the brain cells responsible for your son's problems."

His explanation didn't satisfy Mr. Ren.

"I have been researching this procedure on the Internet," he said quickly, eyes flickering with emotion. "It's very controversial in the West, and hardly ever performed." Mrs. Ren gently squeezed her husband's arm.

Dr. Zhou was taken aback. He stopped walking and turned to face the couple. "I'm telling you, it is only here, in socialist China, where medical care is safe and advancing!" His right hand undulated, emphasizing each word.

"But is the procedure really necessary?" asked Mrs. Ren timidly. "Are there other, less drastic measures we should try first?" She glanced at her husband for approval.

Dr. Zhou's breath became shorter and his face turned red. Suddenly he burst out: "May I remind you that you came to us complaining about your son's withdrawal, his fixation with computer games, his lack of motivation, his blunted emotions, and his antisocial attitudes? We diagnosed him with undifferentiated schizophrenia. Did you know that in the West they abandon people like your son to a short, brutal life on their city streets? Here, we offer your son hope that he can return to a normal, productive life, just like many of my patients!"

Dr. Zhou paused and waited, glad that Dr. Yan had briefed him on the Ren boy's case during yesterday's workout so he could tailor the speech he had just given. Though usually just his prepared talk was enough to shut up bothersome fleas such as the Rens. "Now, is there anything else . . . ?" He looked at them expectantly.

Mr. Ren turned to his wife. She nodded and gave her husband's arm a little shove. From his faded pants pocket, Mr. Ren produced a large, bulging red bag.

"My apologies for doubting you. We want to offer something to compensate you for your troubles."

Dr. Zhou quickly took the red bag and slipped it into his coat pocket. He felt awkward receiving the bribe in full view of the hospital. From the thickness, he figured it was about three thousand yuan—a month's salary for most families in the city.

Since he'd stopped attending banquets, the red bags had

grown fatter. What had previously gone to the restaurant now went to him.

"You are welcome," said Dr. Zhou. "Now if you will please excuse me, I must go save your son from the horrors of schizophrenia."

The couple stopped following him.

Feeling proud of his capacity for handling annoying people, Dr. Zhou strode through the artfully landscaped hospital courtyard, admiring the six-story building he had created. Perhaps that was a slight exaggeration, yet his department of neurosurgery supplied well over half the profits of the hospital, with only a small portion of the staff. He carried many other departments on his back—such as traditional Chinese medicine and geriatrics.

The hospital treated him like a hero. His office was in the best section of the building, on the third floor. By the standards of modern China, he was well paid. Still, without the red bags, he wouldn't have been able to afford his BMW.

After changing into his surgical scrubs, Nurse Ge, a woman with an elegant, egg-shaped face, helped Dr. Zhou into his gown and mask. She led him into the surgery room, holding the door open so that he would not have to touch it.

"This is Ren Shao, age fifteen, diagnosed with undifferentiated schizophrenia," Dr. Yan dutifully reported, his Mandarin marred by a thick country accent. He was extremely thin and a little taller than Dr. Zhou. A big mask covered his face, showing only his thick eyebrows and deep-set eyes. Dr. Yan was in charge of the initial examinations and the prepping of patients for surgery. Two other energetic assistants were in charge of public relations and patient recruitment. Dr. Zhou was pleased that his team ran as smoothly as his BMW.

All except for a little issue concerning Dr. Yan. Dr. Zhou was fully aware that for several months Dr. Yan had been fishing around for a directorship elsewhere. Thanks to his connections, Dr. Zhou was able to keep Dr. Yan grounded for the time being, at least until he could replace him with a new assistant.

Looking upon his patient for the first time, Dr. Zhou nodded. The boy was covered from the neck down with a white sheet. His shaved head made him look older than his age.

Dr. Yan stood near the patient's head, adjusting the cradle and probes used to insert the needles.

"Pleased to meet you, Mr. Ren," Dr. Zhou remarked lightly. Of course, there was no reply from the patient. The anesthetics had already begun working, as expected.

Dr. Zhou examined the CAT scans on the light panel, then watched as a short, plump nurse scrubbed the patient's shaved scalp with an antibiotic solution that gave the pale skin a brownish tint. When the nurse finished, Dr. Yan carefully measured out three locations and marked them with a red pen. He moved the cradle into position and then checked and double-checked the orientation of the probes that would guide the three needles of differing lengths into the patient's brain.

"Dr. Zhou, isn't the mayor's banquet today?" asked Nurse Ge. Her eyes conveyed a knowing smile behind her mask.

Dr. Zhou rechecked all the measurements and the positioning of the probes.

"Hmm. Drill." Dr. Zhou held out his hand. Nurse Ge placed the sterile surgical drill in his right palm.

"Yes!" he remarked over the *wh-i-i-i-i-ne* of the drill. "The thought of it has been giving me nightmares . . ." A meaty, burnt smell wafted through the air. Dr. Zhou pulled the drill out of the skull and then repositioned it over the next red dot. ". . . that my car ran out of gas and I couldn't find a station." *Wh-i-i-i-i-ne.*

"I ended up abandoning it in the middle of the street and had to run across town." *Wh-i-i-i-i-ne.*

"So this morning I filled up my tank."

Everybody dutifully laughed along with him. He handed the drill back to Nurse Ge.

"Let's finish quickly so you have plenty of time to get there," said Dr. Yan cheerfully. He placed an oval tray next to Nurse Ge. On it lay three different lengths of thin needles, each with a yellow note taped below, bearing a number.

Dr. Zhou specialized in treating two forms of schizophrenia. The first was paranoid schizophrenia. He often characterized it as being associated with criminal or actively antisocial behavior. It could involve hallucinations or delusions. A patient might hear voices and act irrationally against society.

The second was undifferentiated, where a person might be withdrawn, depressed, and speak little.

The treatment for either illness was very similar: three holes and three needles of precise increasing lengths heated for sixty seconds to kill microscopic zones within the patient's brain.

Over the years, Dr. Zhou had found that, contrary to his expectations, the paranoid schizophrenics often responded better to a lighter treatment. They required a shallower penetration than those used for the undifferentiated schizophrenics.

As Dr. Zhou picked up the shortest number 1 needle, his cell phone rang. Annoyed, he set down the needle.

Since everything in surgery must be sterile, Dr. Zhou carried his phone inside a disinfected bag that he kept in his gown. He pointed to his right pocket.

Nurse Ge quickly reached for the phone, pressed the answer button through the cloth bag, and held it to his ear.

It was the mayor's assistant.

"Yes, you can count on it. I was just telling everyone how much I am looking forward to the banquet. Now if you would excuse me, I am in the middle of an operation. . . . All right then, good-bye!"

Turning back to the tray, Dr. Zhou picked up a needle again. No one noticed that it was a different, longer needle.

The process went smoothly. In less than two hours, Dr. Zhou was on his way to the restaurant.

It was lunchtime, and hundreds of bicycles mixed with the cars, trucks, and buses on the wide street. Laughing schoolchildren weaved through the throngs of street vendors, pausing now and then to examine their wares. Dr. Zhou was glad he didn't have far to go.

The restaurant was easy to spot. Two red lanterns dangled from its curved tile roof, above two large stone lions guarding the entrance. Dr. Zhou turned his car over to a parking attendant dressed in a yellow mandarin-style shirt and wide trousers.

The mayor and his assistant met Dr. Zhou at the front door, grinning broadly.

"*Xiè xie guāng lín!*—Thank you for coming!" The mayor firmly shook his hand, squinting in the glare of the sun. "I know how busy you are, Dr. Zhou."

The mayor was in his early fifties, dressed in a striped polo shirt and slacks. He had the air of a professional athlete about him. He introduced his young assistant, a nice-looking man in a tan suit. "This is Mr. Lin. He was instrumental in arranging today's special treat."

A hostess in a figure-hugging red *qí páo*, a traditional Chinese dress with a high mandarin collar and side slits, came out. She greeted them warmly and led them inside to the cool, conditioned air. The tantalizing aromas and glimpses of bird's nest soup, hot pots, sizzling dumplings, braised seafood, steamed pork buns, jade green vegetables, and sorghum wine whetted Dr. Zhou's appetite.

Expensively dressed men and women packed the restaurant, laughing and drinking, their chopsticks clattering against the fine china. Waiters and waitresses dashed about, carrying fishheads stuffed with small white balls made from their own flesh; whole roasted hogs with eyeballs replaced by red grapes; egg-white pudding sprinkled with chopped cherries and ants.

As the mayor's party walked by, a few guests paused and stared. One man's mouth hung open. Next to him, a woman with slightly bulging brown eyes and gold hoop earrings froze, her chopsticks holding a golden, crispy lizard in midair. Perhaps they recognized the mayor from his frequent appearances in the media, or the famous brain surgeon.

Dr. Zhou caught sight of a neatly printed sign standing beside a big fish tank.

Today's Specials
"Snake Stew Tienma"—
a remedy for headaches.
"Stir-Fried Pig's Ear"—
enhances concentration and hearing.
"Thousand-Year-Old Egg Congee"—
soothes the respiratory organs.
"Deep-Fried Giant Ants" —
strengthens the immune system.

Of course, the dish he eagerly awaited wasn't—couldn't be—on this list. It was going to be far more exotic than any of these specials.

The hostess turned left and led them down a long, narrow hall decorated with traditional ink-brush landscapes. She stopped at the last door on the right and gestured for them to enter.

A low-hanging chandelier lit the room brightly. Mirrors lined the left wall. To the right, plush gold curtains were tightly closed, absorbing light and blocking noise from the street. An enormous flat-panel TV hung on the rear wall. It stared blankly at a long, black leather couch across the room. Beside the couch a half-open door led to a private bathroom complete with shower.

A small round table stood in the center of the large room. Three places were set, each complete with a tiny teacup, a small bowl, a spoon, and a saucer.

When Dr. Zhou spotted the small hole at the table's center, his heart beat with excitement. Once the men were seated, a beautiful waitress with long legs entered, carrying a copper teakettle with a three-foot-long spout. She poured hot tea into the cups, stopping a split second before the cup would overflow. The fragrance of jasmine permeated the air. The mayor lifted his teacup and gestured to his guest. "Please, please."

Dr. Zhou picked up his cup and sipped.

Long Legs brought over a rectangular wooden tray. With bamboo tongs she gracefully picked up towels folded to resemble spring rolls, and passed them to everyone. Dr. Zhou spread the towel over his face and inhaled the pleasant mint scent.

Until a couple of years ago, he wouldn't have dreamed that there would be a day when he could enjoy this high lifestyle.

Dr. Zhou had grown up in a working-class family. His father, a minor Communist Party member at a midsized leather shoe factory, made little money and had next to no power. But those leather shoes had served well as gifts to get Dr. Zhou into a second-rate medical school. There he had specialized in neurosurgery.

After graduation, despair washed over him like bitter tea. The university assigned him to the Department of Mental Illness at People's Liberation Army Hospital 549. It was the worst job possible for a doctor, so bad he wished he had just gone to work at his father's shoe factory instead of attending medical school. Having to help those crazy people eat and use toilets—the thought still made him shiver.

Then, three years ago, there came an even worse disaster. The government cut the budget of the PLA. The hospital couldn't pay salaries for months at a time. Knowing that in crisis there is opportunity, Dr. Zhou presented a bold plan to the board. He suggested opening the hospital doors to the public—with expanded medical services. The capstone of his plan was to offer special mental-health treatments and promote them through the media.

That was how Dr. Zhou founded the highly profitable department of neurosurgery. Soon he became well known, especially among rich and powerful government officials and businessmen. The steep surgical fee—35,000 yuan, or

$4,500 in U.S. dollars—had also brought him much media attention. And respect.

Sometimes, he couldn't believe that he had survived all those years without "the money for your trouble" in the red bags. Eating cheap buckwheat noodles and plain tofu every day was a distant memory. *Imagine having to live through that all over again.*

Two male waiters walked in, dressed in yellow cotton uniforms meant to imitate farmers' garb. One had a crew cut, the other had his hair dyed red. Together they carried a cage with a live monkey inside. A rancid smell stung Dr. Zhou's nostrils. They should have prepped the monkey before this procedure, he thought scornfully.

The mayor turned to Dr. Zhou. "This young monkey is from the southeastern border. It took my son's friends two days to catch it. Afterward, Mr. Lin arranged for it to be drugged and couriered here in a special case."

"I had to bribe a few flight attendants." Mr. Lin smiled conspiratorially, displaying his straight white teeth. "I heard that live monkey brains are far more potent than dead ones. Supposedly they enhance the diner's alertness, intelligence, and mental agility, not that you two are lacking any of that."

"Have you heard of that, Dr. Zhou?" asked the mayor cajolingly.

"Hmm. Something like that," Dr. Zhou answered. He wanted to study every detail of the preparation of the monkey, yet he could not ignore his host. "I am most impressed by what an exotic delicacy it is."

Long Legs spooned chili-garlic sauce, a mixture of minced red chili peppers, green onions, garlic, and soy sauce, into the saucers on the table. The pungent smell lingered in the air, blocking some of the rank odor coming from the monkey.

The mayor cleared his throat and then said, "My son told me that live monkey brains give the diner supernatural energy. We could all use some of that. After this meal, we can party for days."

The mayor and his assistant laughed heartily.

Dr. Zhou nodded, but his eyes were fixed on the monkey. It appeared to be sleeping on the bottom of the cage. He wondered what type of anesthetic they had used to drug the animal.

The mayor lowered his voice and leaned toward the doctor. "The police told me that they can't release my son until two days before the operation."

Crew Cut slid out the right leaf of the table, exposing a bamboo basket attached underneath. Fascinated, Dr. Zhou watched as Red Hair gingerly removed the monkey from its cage, holding it by the neck. With the monkey in his hands, he kneeled down and leaned under the table.

The mayor continued, "My son said that after he recovers from the operation, he hopes to settle in the United States. Then he'd like to arrange a visit for you."

Dr. Zhou nodded. He would love to visit Las Vegas and

try his luck at a real gambling table. He had a feeling that he would be good at it.

Red Hair pushed the monkey's head through the hole and Crew Cut closed the table with a click. The monkey's chin rested on the table, its body in the basket.

In his heart, Dr. Zhou despised children like the mayor's son. They suffered from a high rate of paranoid schizophrenia. How else could you explain such disruptive behavior as drug using and dealing? Of course, for almost any other crime, even trafficking in foreign vehicles, the mayor's connections could have rescued the boy from trouble. However, the government had no tolerance for drug offenses.

Dr. Zhou had testified that the mayor's son was criminally insane. That it would be cruel and inefficient for the state to execute him. He could cure him, just like many of his other patients who now led productive lives.

Crew Cut left the room; Red Hair began to shave the monkey's head with electric clippers.

Eventually the mayor's son might return home after everybody had forgotten his transgression. Or he might just end up running a fancy restaurant in the United States.

Crew Cut returned, carrying a silver tray holding a small saw and a serving spoon. Dr. Zhou shifted in his chair with anticipation.

As if he guessed what Dr. Zhou was thinking, the mayor stood up and brought over the tray. "Would you like the privilege? No one is more suited for this task than you."

"It will be an honor." Dr. Zhou stood, picking up the saw. He leaned forward, his pudgy belly pressing against the edge of the table. He cut along the monkey's forehead. Blood welled out of the incision.

What he saw disturbed him. The mayor and his assistant were relishing the monkey's mutilation.

Gathering his wits, he continued sawing, and completed a neat line. When done, he let out a quiet sigh and returned to his seat, relieved that his part was over.

"Your reputation as a skilled surgeon is much deserved," said the mayor, smiling approvingly.

Long Legs handed Dr. Zhou a white towel to wipe his hands. He stained it bright red.

Red Hair entered, carrying a pot of hot peanut oil and a ladle. As he held the pot, Crew Cut dipped the ladle into the oil.

Leaning toward Dr. Zhou, Mr. Lin explained eagerly, "Hot oil will augment the flavor."

Crew Cut poured the oil onto the monkey's now-exposed brain. A smell like frying pig fat filled the room. The brain turned from pink to gray as it congealed.

The mayor and his assistant clapped their hands lightly. "Well done! Well done!"

Long Legs scooped portions of the monkey's brain into the three bowls, breaking it into small pieces, like soft tofu. She then spooned some chili-garlic sauce on it before handing the first bowl to Dr. Zhou.

Most of the excitement Dr. Zhou felt had vanished. He broke off a piece with the tip of his spoon and slowly brought the chunk doused with dark sauce to his mouth. Eyes half closed, he let it slip onto his tongue and—was disappointed. The flavor and consistency were akin to soft steamed tofu, with a slight underlying taste of the peanut oil. He should have expected this; the brain is just soft tissue and can't hold much flavor.

But Dr. Zhou was soon shocked by the strong aftertaste. The chili sauce could not conceal the metallic bite. He swallowed hard. His mouth felt like it was coated in blood. Everything about the brain nauseated him.

The mayor and his assistant rolled each bite around in their mouths, relishing it before swallowing—as if eating the freshest tofu. They were discussing something passionately, but Dr. Zhou couldn't care less. As he considered how to excuse himself to go to the bathroom and rinse his mouth, his cell phone rang. He set the bowl down.

"*Wei?*"

"Dr. Zhou? This is Officer Wang." Wang was the chief political officer of the hospital and in charge of daily operations.

"Yes?"

"The boy you operated on today, Ren Shao . . . I'm afraid he died."

"How? When?" Dr. Zhou rose from the table. The taste in his mouth intensified.

"A few minutes ago he suddenly woke up screaming and vomited violently. By the time the nurses reached him he was in convulsions, and died quickly."

Dr. Zhou imagined the boy screaming just as he cut through the monkey's scalp. "I see. I will come immediately." Something welled up in his throat. He tried hard not to throw up.

"No," Officer Wang said flatly. "There is nothing here for you to do. I have already told Dr. Yan to contact the family. You may want to consider taking the day off tomorrow. We can reschedule your operations and get this incident sorted out." Wang hung up.

"Something's come up at the hospital," Dr. Zhou said bluntly. "I need to go."

The mayor and his assistant stood up respectfully, looking concerned. "Sorry you have to go," said the assistant. "We have many more exotic dishes coming."

Dr. Zhou was grateful for the excuse to leave. In fact, he would have said almost anything to avoid taking another bite of monkey brain.

The mayor walked with Dr. Zhou, asking politely about the emergency at the hospital.

"Not so much an emergency as an . . . inconvenience." Dr. Zhou tried to be as vague as possible, but he expected the mayor would find out about the incident soon enough.

"Let me know if there is anything I can do to help. We are counting on you." The mayor patted Dr. Zhou's shoulder.

"Don't worry. I will schedule your son as soon as possible." Dr. Zhou swallowed hard, valiantly fighting the intense nausea. He desperately wished to leave, but the mayor lingered by him outside the restaurant.

"I know you have assured me of this many times, but I feel compelled to ask again about the operation. Are there any risks involved with the surgery?"

Despite the cool air in the restaurant, Dr. Zhou's shirt clung to his back, now drenched in sweat. There was a moment's pause. Dr. Zhou wanted to shout, *Of course there are risks, idiot! It's also risky to deal in heroin, but that didn't stop your son from doing it. If you don't trust me, let him face the death penalty.*

Instead, Dr. Zhou put on his public face and said calmly, avoiding the mayor's eyes, "With cases like your son's, the procedure is of low risk and yields very positive results. You can talk to the city's party secretary, Mr. Liu, or the police chief, Xiao. Their sons had similar symptoms."

Dr. Zhou handed his valet ticket to an approaching attendant and continued, "Both of their sons underwent the same procedure. Secretary Liu's son is now a successful businessman in South America, and Chief Xiao's son owns several Chinese restaurants in California."

"Actually, it was Chief Xiao who recommended you to me. I am sorry to keep asking about this," the mayor said apologetically. The attendant arrived with the bright red BMW.

As Dr. Zhou stepped forward, the mayor grabbed his

elbow. "You understand that he is my only son, and is dear to me despite the trouble he causes."

Dr. Zhou nodded, and got into his car. The mayor discreetly slid a thick red bag into Dr. Zhou's suit pocket.

Dr. Zhou's apartment was located in a new-money neighborhood with wide streets and green lawns. When he arrived home, there was a message on his answering machine from Officer Wang. The parents had taken their son's death badly. Officer Wang asked him to meet for lunch the next day at the hospital to discuss the situation.

Dr. Zhou abruptly cut off the message. Getting rid of the brain taste was much more important. He emptied a bottle of mouthwash and brushed his teeth over and over without success.

It was a long, miserable night. The taste kept him awake, and when he finally dozed off, he was awakened by crying. In the faint light he thought he glimpsed the Ren boy, holding the monkey, floating along the wall. Both had shaved heads and blood dripping down their faces.

Dr. Zhou's heart pounded like a snared deer's. He sat up and turned on the light. Nothing! He lay back, leaving the lights on, fighting to keep his eyes open, but he drifted off. Suddenly, something that felt like a small, furry hand brushed across his forehead. He leaped out of bed, screaming hysterically.

Staggering from room to room, he turned on all the lights and television sets. The TV in the bedroom was playing a kung fu movie. The huge plasma screen in the living room was showing a documentary about South America.

Lulled by the distracting sounds of clashing swords and growling lions, he closed his eyes. A soothing male voice speaking in perfect Mandarin drifted from the TV.

"Now, let's take a closer look at the amazing howler monkey. These unique animals are distinguished by their loud howls, which they use to communicate over long distances."

Horrifying howls echoed through the room, forcing Dr. Zhou to open his eyes. The kung-fu fighters had been replaced by dozens of red-faced monkeys. He grabbed the remote and changed the channel. A monkey, swinging a long stick, stared back at him. It was a remake of the old Chinese classic *The Monkey King*.

For hours, Dr. Zhou rapidly pressed the remote buttons. Monkeys were on every channel! A few times he thought he saw the Ren boy float by, holding a monkey. He backed up to look for the channel again, only to find red-faced monkeys fighting over bananas. Finally, exhausted and soaked in sweat, he let out a scream of frustration, turned off the TV, and threw the remote at it.

By morning, the disgusting taste had intensified. Even his soy milk tasted like brains. He spat constantly, trying to

clear his mouth. As he brushed his teeth for the seventh time, the phone rang.

"*Wei?*"

"Hello, Dr. Zhou!" It was Officer Wang. Without waiting for a reply, he continued. "I have bad news. The boy's father has submitted a story to every paper in town. We think he wants to trigger a government investigation. This will keep me busy all day. So let's have lunch tomorrow, all right? *Zài jiàn*—Good-bye!" He hung up.

Officer Wang was a short, solid man with a potbelly and a bald patch on his crown. When he met Dr. Zhou the next day at the hospital's cafeteria, he was surprised by the doctor's appearance. Unshaven and rumpled, he reeked of sweat and an odd mint odor. His beady eyes were bloodshot, with dark pouches spreading under them. The wrinkles at the corners of his eyes had grown deeper and thicker.

It was a little before the lunch break and only a few staff members sat around the white, cloth-covered tables. Officer Wang guided Dr. Zhou through the cafeteria line as he talked.

"No worries! We have nipped that filthy journalist's efforts. After two editors informed us yesterday, I called the other papers. Fortunately, we have good relations with the media. Only one small paper dared to publish the story, and even then we were able to reduce it to little more than a small piece of tofu on a back page."

Officer Wang placed a bowl of rice on each of their trays

as Dr. Zhou blankly stared at the space beyond the man's shoulder.

"We are lucky that one of my old army buddies is the political officer for *Ocean News*." Officer Wang selected a cup of wonton soup for himself, and a cup of egg drop for Dr. Zhou. "My friend is arranging an early retirement for the boy's father. Would you like some garlic fish? Here, how about some steamed tofu with chili-garlic sauce?"

"No!" shouted Dr. Zhou. He blocked the dish from his tray with a shaking hand. Officer Wang paused, studying Dr. Zhou's haggard face for a moment before placing the tofu dish and a small bowl of dark sauce on his own tray. He led the way to an empty table.

Dr. Zhou followed, a loud cough racking his body. He cleared his throat and spat on the floor. After grinding the spit into the carpet with the sole of his brown leather shoe, he sat across from Officer Wang.

Officer Wang suppressed his shock at Dr. Zhou's behavior. Taking a moment to collect himself, he continued. "In a way, it's fortunate that the Rens are intellectuals. Remember the village boy that was here last year? That kid didn't even die! When he left, he could still use one hand and yet the whole village showed up and wrecked the lobby of the hospital. Bunch of hooligans if you ask me."

Dr. Zhou listlessly stirred his soup.

"We will have to hold a hospital board meeting to review

this unfortunate incident." Using the tip of his porcelain spoon, Officer Wang broke the tofu into small pieces and then spooned some sauce onto it. "I think we can proceed through it quickly, though, and you can probably be back on the job by next week. How does that sound?" he asked, smiling.

Dr. Zhou muttered something and his lips twisted into a puerile grin.

Officer Wang took a spoonful of tofu and rolled it around in his mouth, relishing it before swallowing. "Eat, eat. Don't let your food get cold," he urged.

Dr. Zhou took a small, tentative sip of the egg drop soup.

"By the way, how was the mayor's banquet?"

"*Ploo!*" Dr. Zhou spat the soup into Officer Wang's face. "Why are you feeding me monkey brain!" he screamed. Officer Wang jumped from his chair, knocking it over. Stunned, he wiped his face with his sleeve.

Dr. Zhou stood up, violently sweeping the dishes off the table, his face twisted in horror. Tofu, soup, and rice flew all about. "The boy is not dead. He's right behind you! Why are you lying to me?" He waved his arms wildly. "Take him away. Stop his bleeding!"

Two large orderlies at a nearby table rushed to wrestle Dr. Zhou to the floor.

Later that afternoon, Officer Wang called for an emergency meeting of the Communist Party review board. It took two hours to evaluate the case. The next day, Officer Wang summarized the board's decisions to the staff of the neuro-surgery department.

"A patient in Dr. Zhou's care suffered unfortunate complications. This event appears to have triggered Dr. Zhou's mental collapse as, shortly afterwards, he began to exhibit symptoms of severe paranoid schizophrenia, including delusions and violent behavior. Due to the enormous contributions Dr. Zhou has made to this hospital, the directors have decided to give him the best treatment the hospital can provide. The cost shall be deducted from his future pay.

"In the meantime, Dr. Yan will assume directorship of the department of neurosurgery. We can all hope that under Dr. Yan's expert care, Dr. Zhou will recover sufficiently to resume a productive life and return to his post."

Whispering broke out among the staff. There was a brief smattering of applause, and all eyes turned to Dr. Yan—who stood and bowed slightly.

"Thank you for your confidence in me," he said timidly, sweat glistening across his brow. "As you may know, I've already begun treatment for Dr. Zhou. He has violently refused all food and water. He also tried to poison himself by eating the soap in the washroom." Dr. Yan glanced at Officer Wang, who nodded his approval.

"As a result, I ordered him to be heavily sedated and put on an IV to keep him hydrated. We will force-feed him until ablative surgery can be performed." He wiped his forehead with his sleeve. "With our track record for treating patients like Dr. Zhou, I believe his prognosis is good."

"Thank you for your report." Officer Wang stood up. "Everyone back to work. And remember, let's keep this to ourselves!" The staff exchanged glances as they walked out.

A few days later, on a sunny afternoon, Dr. Yan glided into the surgical room in a very good mood. He'd spent the morning visiting a car dealership. It wouldn't be long before he could afford the down payment on a new BMW sports car.

His promotion had come at a fortuitous time. Under Dr. Zhou, he had expected little chance for advancement in either title or income. Now he had everything.

He looked at his former superior and colleague on the gurney, sedated and shaved, his eyes tightly closed, lips dried and cracked. Dr. Yan couldn't find any of the old confidence in that flabby face.

It didn't take long for Dr. Yan to drill three holes and insert the first needle. The tip of the second needle was heating up when his cell phone rang. Nurse Ge took the phone from Dr. Yan's pocket and held it against his ear.

"Wei?"

"Hello, Dr. Yan? This is Mr. Feng from the BMW dealership."

"Oh! Yes?" Dr. Yan replied cheerfully.

"Would you like your Z4 convertible in titanium silver? Or perhaps Montego blue?"

"What do you mean?" Dr. Yan sounded confused. "I told you I need to save up for the down payment."

"The president of People's Bank has covered the down payment for your Z4. His sister is a new patient of yours. Do you know who she is?"

Dr. Yan laughed delightedly. "Of course I do! She is the one charged with manufacturing methamphetamines." He gestured animatedly with his arm. As Dr. Yan chatted happily with the salesman, no one noticed the timer for the needle sweeping past the sixty-second mark.

"Montego blue sounds nice—but I like red. Yes, bright red!"

Three months later:

To Officer Wang's surprise, an article by the dead boy's father appeared in *The Beijing News*. He'd never dreamed that the father had connections in Beijing.

When major newspapers across China syndicated the article, the hospital suspended everyone in Dr. Yan's neurosurgery department without pay.

Officer Wang resigned after a local station broadcasted a story on the evening news:

"Following a recent article in *The Beijing News* about corrupt and incompetent medical practices, the central government has organized an investigative team and is drafting strict regulations and a review process on brain surgery for treating schizophrenia. . . ."

The story ended with footage of a flabby-faced, middle-aged man with a lame right leg walking around PLA Hospital 549. His lips were dried and cracked. Every sixty seconds he spat into a small bucket that he carried.

TREATMENT OF MENTAL ILLNESS, ECONOMIC REFORMS, AND MONKEY BRAINS

Chinese society has always considered mental illness a taboo and shameful topic. The families look upon the patients as a disgrace and are willing to take whatever steps necessary to cure them. The year I entered university, one of my high school classmates suddenly took a long trip, according to her family. Later, I found out that she had suffered from depression after failing the university entrance exam. Her family had sent her off to a mental hospital.

During China's recent transition to a free-market economy, the health-care system went through upheaval and reform. The central government shed its responsibility for formulating policy and financing public health care. The system became market-oriented and commercialized. Financial autonomy gave health providers and hospitals incentives to maximize revenues. It became an unspoken rule that patients give doctors red bags (bribes) to "do their best," and some hospitals even deny treatment for patients who cannot afford to pay the high medical fees.

Many Asian cultures have long viewed the consumption of still-living animal flesh as a special delicacy. It is also interpreted as an act of machismo or daring, and greeted with a certain fascinated revulsion. More important, the diners believe that this practice will bequeath upon them great physical and mental benefits. For example, the fresh blood of a snake boosts the immune system, an entire live scorpion augments physical strength, and monkey brains heighten mental agility and provide supernatural energy.

Other exotic delicacies include shark's fins, jellyfish, pig's tails, and bear paws. There is a saying that the Chinese eat everything with four legs except the table. I would agree that no other culture is as resourceful and creative in making delicacies out of the most unlikely ingredients.

TOFU WITH CHILI-GARLIC SAUCE

If you don't have a steamer, set tofu on a heatproof plate on top of a heatproof bowl. Place it in the bottom of a pot filled with two inches of water. Cover and steam. There should be adequate water in the pot, but it shouldn't touch the tofu.

Makes 4 servings.

½ cup soy sauce

2 tablespoons lemon juice

2 tablespoons rice vinegar

1 red chili pepper, minced

2 cloves garlic, minced

1 scallion, minced

2 teaspoons sesame oil

2 teaspoons honey

1 package (18 ounces) water-packed soft or silken tofu

▣ Combine all the ingredients except the tofu in a small bowl. Cover and refrigerate for 30 minutes to allow flavors to blend.

▣ Drain the tofu and gently invert it onto a cutting board.

▣ Pat the tofu dry with towels. Cut it into 8 equal cubes by first cutting the block into 2 sheets, then cutting both sheets in half and then in quarters. Place the tofu in a single layer in a heat-resistant dish.

▦ Place the dish in a bamboo or vegetable steamer. Steam the tofu, covered, for 5 minutes. Carefully lift the dish from the steamer. Spoon some sauce over the tofu. Serve warm.

Long-Life Noodles

Just BEFORE DAWN, Master Ma, in his yellow robe and matching felt boots, gazed serenely at the 130 monks lined up before the gate of Wu Jing Temple. He was a tall man with a high forehead, slightly stooped, wearing a small cloth backpack. In a deep voice devoid of emotion he said, "It has been an honor to lead this temple since it reopened, and now I must go to seek purification. Stay loyal to the Communist Party. Be diligent in your political studies, and remain true to Buddha's teachings."

All the monks pressed their hands together and bowed to him. With a curt nod of dismissal, he strode through the gate and headed down the long stone path that led to the village at the foot of the mountain. A moment later, slapping footsteps came up behind him. He glanced back and saw Master Chen, a short man with small shoulders and deep-set shifty eyes.

Master Chen was a senior member of the Communist Party with a lot of *guàn xì*—political connections. Even though Master Ma had appointed Master Chen as his temporary replacement, he had never been fond of him.

Chen carried a basket tucked under one arm. "May I walk with you for a while?" he asked.

Ma shrugged and hid his distaste behind the serene mask he always wore in public. He slowed down so Chen could keep pace. As they rounded the corner and passed the temple's terraced vegetable gardens, a cool mist engulfed them. Thick clouds filtered the first rays of sunlight. A few birds chirped in the distance. They were completely alone.

Chen stopped in front of Ma. "Dear master, I am going to miss you. Here is some food grown in our gardens, including your favorite shiitake mushrooms."

Ma's eyebrows arched in surprise. "Thank you." He bowed slightly as he accepted the basket.

Ma picked out a sugar pea and popped it into his mouth. "Mmm, only in unpolluted mountains like these does the food taste so good." He reached for a plump mushroom. "Ow!" He quickly jerked back his hand, dropping the basket. Spilled vegetables rolled down the dirt path. A small black snake whipped out of the basket and slithered into the brush.

Blood welled up from two deep puncture wounds.

"That's a three-steps snake," Chen sneered viciously. "You won't get farther than three steps before you die."

Fiery pain swept up Ma's arm. He looked at Chen, eyes filled with disbelief before his knees gave way.

As Ma writhed in agony on the ground, Chen squatted and tore Ma's pack from his back. There he found the two things he wanted: Ma's chop—a seal carved from stone, used as a signature—and a bankbook for an account that held millions of yuan.

"You think I believed you about your so-called pilgrimage? I know about your mistresses and expensive cars in the coastal cities."

Spasms shook Ma's body. A guttural growl rose in his throat that quickly turned into a choked gurgle.

Chen stuffed the seal and bankbook in his jacket pocket. "Now I will enjoy the money you have stolen, because you won't need it. You know what else I am going to do?" His smile grew wider. "I will take all the money from the monastery's accounts, and blame that on you, too."

Blood oozed from Ma's nose, eyes, and ears, and burst from his mouth. He reached out toward Chen.

Horrified, Chen took a few steps back.

Ma gave out a low moaning cry and stopped moving. His dead eyes stared at the narrow path stretching down the mountain toward the ocean.

Chen dragged Ma to a burial spot he'd already chosen.

Two days later, Master Chen reported to his superiors in Beijing that Master Ma had stolen millions of yuan. After recovering from the shock, the senior monks reported this to the central government, but the police couldn't locate Master Ma. Master Chen was permanently in charge of Wu Jing Temple.

On a cool October day, the two red doors to the monastery remained closed. Inside, the monks milled around, preparing for Master Chen's fiftieth birthday celebration.

Since Master Chen had become the head monk six months earlier, rumors had spread like wildfire in a dry field. One version had it that Master Ma had stolen enough money to last him two lifetimes. Some scoffed. As if anyone who stole that kind of money could hide from the Communist government for very long.

With the growing number of newly rich in China, the temple received many large donations from local residents, as well as from patrons overseas. More money and gifts poured in every week. Master Chen now had millions stashed in secret offshore accounts. He had set up his two mistresses with luxurious lifestyles, providing them with expensive cars and homes in newly rich neighborhoods.

When the great brass bell tolled at five that evening, the junior monks in the temple pushed open the heavy front doors. The long line of patrons hushed as Master Chen came out to greet them. Visitors flipped on their camcorders to record this historic moment. Master Chen stood at the great entrance in a bright yellow robe, next to two larger-than-life statues of Buddha. With his hands pressed together in front of him, Master Chen bowed low to the crowd.

The guests all carried gifts: incense, fruit, and—most important of all—the small red paper bags that contained good-luck money. They were eager to pay their respects to the head monk, hoping that he might include the names of their dead loved ones in a daily chant, or even hold a special ceremony to bless their souls.

Master Chen graciously accepted the red bags, slipping them into his two deep pockets. Cong, the youngest monk, along with six others, humbly stood beside him, recording the names and gifts of the guests. They placed the larger gifts inside two capacious handwoven wicker baskets. Like busy ants, they ran back and forth to the temple to empty them once they filled up.

In the storage room, when a bag of ginseng roots burst open, Cong stuffed a handful into his inner pocket. He had learned from other young monks to pick up loose items when the opportunity arose. Cong had joined the temple on his sixteenth birthday. He and his family had thought it was a smart way to leave the poor countryside. The government offered young monks free room and board, plus fifty yuan (about $7) a month. But Cong quickly discovered that life here was even worse. The senior monks worked them like animals and he got less to eat than at home.

As daylight faded and the full moon ascended, the junior monks lit two hundred red lanterns. Columns of incense burned in huge basins outside the front gate. From a distance, the red glow and smoke gave the illusion that the temple was on fire.

Master Chen sat at a large, round banquet table in the center of the courtyard, accompanied by nine prestigious guests. Encircling them, lesser guests gathered at rough-hewn limestone tables and pine benches.

Once the guests had settled in, a long column of monks dressed in red and golden robes marched into the courtyard. They quietly chanted prayers and blessings as they tapped sticks against small wooden drums. A gentle breeze carried the pungent smells of onion, garlic, and sesame from the kitchen, mixing with the muskiness of burning incense and the fragrance of the chrysanthemums around the garden.

Led by Master Lung, the kitchen master, a long line of monks filed into the courtyard, carrying lavish dishes. There was sautéed beef, roasted sausages, golden crispy fish, and "drunken" shrimp steeped in old medicinal sorghum wine—all made with soybeans, mushrooms, seaweed, and other vegetables and seasonings. Due to their religious beliefs, the Buddhists did not eat meat, so they had become very skilled at creating vegetarian substitutes. Guests cried out with delight, commenting on the authentic look of the vegetarian meats and seafood; the elegant garnish of lily bulbs, lotus seeds, wolfberries, and flowers made from yellow radishes, orange carrots, and green onions.

When Master Lung set a big bowl of long-life noodles in front of Chen, all eyes focused upon him. Courtesy dictated that no one eat until the host had finished his long-life noodles. Chen took his first bite.

"Delicious! Absolutely delicious!" Chen exclaimed. He lowered his head deeper into the big bowl and took another bite. "It's so flavorful!" he cried with joy.

A proud smile spread across Master Lung's face.

"Wonderful flavor!" murmured Chen, greedily chewing a piece of soy beef. He slurped down noodles as fast as his chopsticks could move.

A brilliant streak of lightning flared across the cloudless sky. Master Chen dropped the half-full porcelain bowl. It shattered on the slate paving stones as he clutched his stomach and gave a loud groan. Blood oozed from his mouth, nose, eyes, and ears. Spasms swept his body. He flailed about, knocking his chair over and spilling the dishes on the ornate table. A deep gurgle rose from his throat. Like water exploding from a burst pipe, a mixture of chewed-up noodles and blood shot from his mouth.

The courtyard erupted in turmoil.

"Get a doctor!"

"What's wrong?"

"Poison! Someone poisoned his noodles!"

People crowded around Chen. A senior monk held Chen's head in his arms and wailed hysterically, "He is dead! He is dead!"

Police Chief Xiong, a middle-aged, stocky man with a few pockmarks on his straight nose, was among the guests. He pulled his cell phone from his designer suit and called his office. In less than ten minutes, a truck full of heavily armed policemen arrived and surrounded the temple. After questioning everyone, the police took Master Chen's body with them.

In less than a week, Chief Xiong received the report from the crime lab. Combining it with his interviews, he was sure he knew who had killed the headmaster. Master Lung was in charge of the banquet, and as the only other Communist Party member in the temple, he was an obvious successor to the desirable position of head monk. Yet one thing puzzled Xiong. If Lung had wanted to poison Master Chen, why had he done it in public, when it would be so easily traced to him?

Chief Xiong returned to the temple with four policemen. They found Master Lung in the central hall of worship, sitting on a cushion that resembled a golden lotus. With his hands joined in prayer, he chanted in a steady, dull drone to a large statue of Buddha.

Two policemen roughly grabbed Master Lung's arms, heaved him up, and swung him around to face Chief Xiong.

"What have I done?" exclaimed Lung.

Chief Xiong began with his favorite interrogation technique: "We know everything. Confess, and we will be lenient with your punishment. Denial will increase its severity."

Master Lung was a grand fellow: muscular, broad-shouldered, and square-jawed. He regained his composure quickly and looked straight at Xiong. "If you think I killed Chen, you are wrong. Chen and I were friends and roommates at the Communist Party Leader College."

Ignoring his answer, Chief Xiong ordered Lung to list all the ingredients that had gone into the long-life noodles.

"Green-tea buckwheat noodles, vegetarian beef, sesame paste, garlic, chilies, ginger . . ." Lung listed them slowly.

"What about fresh mushrooms?" Xiong interrupted.

"Oh yes! When I was looking for scallions, I found a patch of fresh shiitake mushrooms."

"Show me these mushrooms," Chief Xiong ordered.

Master Lung took a long breath to calm himself, and then replied, "All right." He led Xiong and his men to the far section of the garden, in the shadow of the mountains. Cong and a group of curious monks followed.

"Here they are!" Master Lung pointed at the thriving patch of mushrooms standing in the late afternoon light. They looked just like ordinary shiitakes, with their dark brown caps and thick stems.

"That's odd." Chief Xiong touched one with his fingers.

Master Lung squatted down next to him. "What is?"

"Shiitakes don't grow out of the ground like that. They

grow on logs." Xiong turned and looked at Lung with suspicion. "You're the head chef. You didn't know that?"

"I am a chef, not a farmer," Master Lung replied huffily. He picked a mushroom with a thick cap and continued, "Well, it is strange. We haven't had enough rain for mushrooms to grow."

Chief Xiong ordered Cong and the othes young monks to fetch shovels from a nearby straw hut. The policemen started to dig. The soil was dark and soft, and their shovels quickly struck something other than dirt. "Careful now!" ordered Xiong.

Gradually an outline appeared. A horrid, rotting smell rose up.

"It's a body!" one young policeman with protruding ears shouted. Another retched in disgust.

Chief Xiong urged them on. "Keep digging! He isn't going to bite you!"

Reluctantly, they continued. Soon they fully uncovered the body. Worms and insects had taken up residence within the bloated stomach. Mushrooms grew from its belly, legs, and hollow eye sockets. Two stems even grew from its ears.

The remains of a yellow monk's robe clung to the body. On his chest rested a small backpack.

"That is Master Ma's backpack," Cong shouted. "Something is wrong here."

No one paid attention to Cong, their eyes fixed on the four policemen as they lifted the rotten body out of the hole.

"Move back! Move back!" Master Lung suddenly shouted.

Where the body had lain, a den of hundreds of small snakes coiled together, writhing about.

"These are three-steps snakes." Master Lung pushed back Cong, who was standing near the edge of the hole. "If bitten by one, you won't get farther than three steps."

Chief Xiong shook his finger at Master Lung. "Interesting you know so much about snakes. Arrest him!" he ordered.

Two policemen grabbed Lung and clamped handcuffs around his wrists.

Master Lung shouted, "Why me? It's obvious the ghost of Master Ma used his corpse to convey the snake poison into the mushrooms, in a revenge strike from his grave!"

"Perhaps," said Chief Xiong with a wicked grin. "But I would look stupid if I accused a ghost in my report, wouldn't I? Someone has to pay for this murder!"

That winter the innocent Master Lung was executed together with two other men; one had stolen fifty bicycles and the other had been selling counterfeit baby formula.

When news spread of the deaths involving Wu Jing Temple, pilgrims and tourists stopped visiting. They said corruption had overrun the temple and it was no longer holy. Donations tapered off and stopped. Eventually, all the monks left because there weren't enough offerings to keep them fed. Once again, Wu Jing Temple was abandoned. Cong didn't want to return to the countryside, so he traded his monk's robes for the uniform of Country Bob's Chicken. The pay was better and he also got to eat his fill of leftover orders.

Locals confirm that when the moon is full, you can see Master Ma with a bowl of noodles in hand, chasing Master Chen around the temple, crying out, "Eat your noodles! Finish your long-life noodles!"

Buddhist Temples, Offerings, and Vegetarian Dishes

Buddhism is one of the most widely practiced religions in China. Buddhist temples can be found in almost every town and city. During the Cultural Revolution the government banned all religious practices, and monasteries were destroyed or closed.

When China reopened its borders to the West, thousands of loyal religious Chinese expatriates desperately requested that the government restore and reopen the famous monasteries. The patrons hoped to find spiritual pureness within. In exchange, they promised to invest millions of yuan—the Chinese currency—into the local economy, in factories, high-rises, schools, restaurants, and shopping malls.

These offers enticed the government. It assigned a large workforce of craftsmen to duplicate the original beauty of the monasteries. The laborers restored the ornate carvings as well as the ceramic shingles on the roofs, replaced the rotten oak floors, refurnished the grand rooms, and widened the long stone paths that led to the sites of worship, often on mountain plateaus. Within years, many monasteries returned to their former glory.

Once opened, they were crowded with pilgrims and tourists from far and near. From the bottom of a mountain, approaching travelers could smell incense burning and hear the incessant chanting of prayers year-round. Worshipers sit on lotus-blossom cushions to pray because in Buddhism, the lotus is a symbol of purity, love, and compassion.

Some local governments issued restrictions: monks had to engage in weekly political studies; the monastery had to grow a portion of its own food; and, most important, the head monk had to be a member of the Communist Party.

In 2006, I took a cruise down the Yangtze River and visited many monasteries along the way. At one famous temple, located high up a mountain, I spotted an old monk counting a thick bundle of cash behind a large statue of Buddha, paying no attention to the worshipers out front.

Across the courtyard in the main hall, a group of middle-aged women chanted with hundreds of monks. I was told they were rich overseas Chinese who had paid the monastery to pray for their deceased loved ones. The grand total for a three-day ceremony was 5,000 U.S. dollars, about 40,000 yuan, a substantial amount considering that the average Chinese family makes around 3,000 yuan a month. I learned that the head monk was one of the wealthiest men in the city. Intrigued, I did further research about corruption in Buddhist temples, which led to this story.

Although I am not a Buddhist, I have visited many famous monasteries across China, because I enjoy the food cooked by the monks and served at restaurants in the temples. The delicious imitation meat, fish, and chicken dishes they create out of vegetables, seaweed, and soy always amaze me.

Long-Life Noodles

Instead of cake, the Chinese serve noodles at birthday celebrations to symbolize a long, happy life. Use the longest noodles you can find for this recipe.

Makes 4 servings.

8 ounces fresh or dry rice noodles or thin spaghetti

3 tablespoons olive oil

2 teaspoons fresh ginger, peeled and minced

2 cloves garlic, minced

1 cup fresh shiitake mushrooms, cut into 1-inch-wide strips (optional)

8 ounces flavored baked tofu, cut into 1-inch-wide strips

½ cup carrots, cut into match-sized sticks

½ cup seeded red bell pepper, cut into match-sized sticks

2 tablespoons soy sauce

4 scallions, cut diagonally into thin, 2-inch-long slices

Salt and pepper to taste

1 teaspoon sesame oil

¼ cup candied walnuts or other nuts

▧ Cook the noodles according to the package directions. Drain and rinse with cold water to prevent sticking. Set aside.

■ Heat a wok or large pan over medium heat. Add the oil and swirl to coat. Add the ginger and garlic. Stir-fry until fragrant, about 30 seconds. Add mushrooms and tofu and stir-fry for 2 minutes.

■ Add carrots and pepper. Stir-fry for 1 minute or until carrots soften. Mix in the noodles, soy sauce, and scallions. Stir occasionally until noodles are heated through, about 2 minutes. Season with salt and pepper.

■ Stir in sesame oil. Toss to combine and top with walnuts. Serve warm.

Egg Stir-Fried Rice

"HURRY! HURRY! MR. YUE IS DYING!"

Old Housekeeper Ting's shrill voice rang through the gloomy, silent house, awakening everyone. Outside, the bitter fall wind whipped through the dark sky. Dead leaves scratched across the courtyard's paving stones. Mr. Yue's fourteen-year-old daughter, Fong, ran to her father's bedside. Mr. Yue blinked at his beautiful daughter and released one last, long, rattling breath. His dead eyes remained open. Fong buried her face in her hands and cried in shaking sobs.

Fong's young and beautiful stepmother, Madame Peng, stood quietly in the shadows of the hallway, where no one could see the slight smile on her elegant porcelain face.

Mr. Yue had married Madame Peng many years after Fong's mother died in childbirth. Before their marriage,

Madame Peng showed great interest in becoming a loving stepmother. This made Mr. Yue very happy, for he cherished his precious daughter with all his heart and wanted her to be treated well.

However, after the wedding Madame Peng exposed her true nature. She spent Mr. Yue's wealth on extravagant dinner parties. When he was not around, she mistreated the servants and was especially cruel to Fong. With the slightest excuse, she would say, "Sweet little thing, you need time for yourself," and send Fong to her room, often forcing her to stay there all day without food or water.

Fong attempted to reason with her stepmother, but Madame Peng always found ways to outsmart her. Mr. Yue had tried to temper Madame Peng's behavior, doing his best to protect Fong. Now that he was gone, all the servants wondered who would look out for his daughter.

Leaving no time for mourning, Madame Peng assembled the entire staff in the banquet hall. She sat on Mr. Yue's high wooden chair, which stood on a raised platform and was heavily padded with silk cushions. Fong stood in a corner of the room. Through misted eyes, she stared at her father's life-size portrait where it hung above Madame Peng's new "throne." Tears streamed down her pale cheeks like a broken string of pearls.

Madame Peng hushed the twenty whispering servants with a wave of her white silk handkerchief. "From now on, I am the master of the house. Anyone who disobeys me will be severely punished." Madame Peng's almond eyes fixed on Fong with a venomous stare.

Housekeeper Ting, a small man, glanced at the other servants, and then eyed Fong with worry. He had worked at the house since before Fong was born and loved her as if she were his own child. He had often smuggled food and drink to her room during Madame Peng's punishments.

"We have long days ahead of us. Now go back to bed, and get up an hour early tomorrow morning." Madame Peng waved her handkerchief toward the door. The servants and Fong drifted from the room.

Early the next morning, Madame Peng called the household together again. Teacup in hand, she looked down upon them from her high seat. "My dear husband shall have the finest funeral this village has ever seen. We shall follow all the old traditions. Fong, you will have the honor of showing your love and devotion to your father. I will allow you to accompany him through eternity."

The servants gasped in shock. Madame Peng smiled, showing two deep dimples on her red cheeks.

"No!" wailed Fong. "That custom is no longer followed. You just want to get rid of me!"

Faithful old Housekeeper Ting lowered his head and said, "Please, Madame, Fong is right. That tradition is not practiced anymore—"

Madame Peng ignored his plea and raised her voice. "Take her away and prepare her!"

The servants looked at one another. No one moved.

"Have you all gone deaf?" Madame Peng's face turned the color of pork liver. She threw her teacup onto the stone floor. It shattered, splashing tea across the bare feet of servants standing before her.

Finally, two young servants slunk toward Fong, staring at the floor to avoid her eyes. Fong pushed them away.

"Following in the same tradition, I have one request. I don't want to die hungry. Let me have one last meal!" Tears streamed down her pale, rigid face.

A smile creased Madame Peng's face as her hazel eyes widened and her voice grew more nasal. "Certainly we will have a feast, but not for you. You can't eat before the funeral. You must be pure when you are buried."

"Excuse me, Madame." Housekeeper Ting dropped down on his knees. "Please grant Fong her wish. So she will not become a hungry ghost."

All the servants dropped down on their knees, begging that Fong's request be granted.

Madame Peng rose from her chair, stepped off the platform, and moved close to the kneeling servants. "You all dare to challenge my orders?"

The room turned deathly quiet.

"The answer is NO. Now go prepare for the funeral."

Fong wept in despair as Housekeeper Ting led her away.

As soon as the servants were outside the room, they whispered among themselves.

"No good will come of this. She'll return for food," said an old lady with a hunched back.

"I just hope if poor Fong turns into a hungry ghost, she won't come back to haunt us," said a young servant with two long pigtails.

"Of course not," said the old lady, wiping her eyes with her sleeves. "We are not the ones doing her harm."

"There is nothing we can do for her, poor girl," said a long-faced cook.

Back in the dining hall, Madame Peng hugged herself. Perhaps she should have let Fong have her feast. A hungry ghost would be a horrible thing. She shivered. No. She could not change her mind now. Otherwise the servants would think they could pull the whiskers of the tiger whenever they pleased. Besides, what harm could the ghost of a girl like Fong do?

The next morning, walking alongside Mr. Yue's black coffin, servants carried Fong in a palanquin to her father's tomb. The funeral band and mourners followed behind, dressed in white, the color of grief. The gloomy dirge and mournful cries cut through the chill fall morning. Villagers crowded along both sides of the street, murmuring.

Fong was dressed in silk the color of moonlight. Her long black hair had been combed and perfumed. No one could see under her flowing garments the knots that bound her to the bamboo chair.

Everyone averted their eyes from the jade bit that protruded from her lips. Madame Peng had secured it with silk cords tied behind her head to prevent her from eating.

The procession halted at the grave site. Fong glared at her stepmother. Her reddened eyes flamed with hatred. Slowly, the servants carried Fong into the tomb and placed her in a coffin next to her father's. Madame Peng didn't leave the graveyard until the servants had nailed Fong's coffin shut and sealed the heavy stone door to the tomb with cement.

The day after the funeral, Madame Peng began to host a series of banquets, each more lavish than the last.

The sixth feast, on the sixth day following the funeral, was to be the largest the village had ever seen. That morning Madame Peng was astonished to find out that over half her servants were gone.

"They left in the middle of the night," reported Housekeeper Ting. "No one in the village is willing to take their places."

Furious, Madame Peng spent the rest of the day pressing the remaining servants into preparing for that night's banquet. She barely had time to pause for tea.

Rain began as guests dressed in white arrived at the

brightly lit banquet hall. Large funeral wreaths and white banners with black calligraphy flanked the red wooden door.

By the time servants carried in covered steam baskets and trays, a terrible storm raged outside. Flames bobbed wildly on thick white candles. Dark shadows danced on the walls like puppets.

As the last of the trays were placed on the table, Madame Peng stood. "Dear guests, please enjoy this humble dinner to honor my dear, departed husband." With a flourish, she lifted the cover off the largest tray.

It was empty!

Madame Peng's face turned as white as her silk handkerchief. She lifted another lid and then another. All the baskets and trays were empty. "This is some trick—"

"The hungry ghost ate the food!" a stout middle-aged man interrupted, horror dripping from his voice.

"No!" protested Madame Peng. "It's a trick, a bad joke played by a few of my unfaithful servants!"

"This big storm . . . it is a sign a ghost has come," a gray-haired woman with missing teeth said in a high-pitched voice. She stood up to leave.

"You shouldn't have buried that poor girl alive." An old man pointed his finger at Madame Peng. He picked up his cane and hobbled toward the door. "It's bad luck to be here!" he muttered.

All the guests rushed out into the stormy night, murmuring

nervously about horrible things to come. The cook and the other servants swarmed out to see what all the commotion was about.

Madame Peng threw the trays and baskets at her staff. "Who did this? Who?"

The servants cowered in terror. Each pleaded innocence.

Housekeeper Ting knelt before his enraged mistress. His forehead touched the floor. "It's not our fault. It is Fong's hungry ghost! You must believe us!"

Madame Peng paused, her hands twisting at her white scarf. "All of you!" She pointed at the terrified servants. "Gather up lanterns and tools. Go with me to the graveyard! I will show you that there is no ghost. Then I shall extract your confessions!"

By the time they arrived at the graveyard, the wind had slowed down and only small drops of rain fell. It didn't take long for the servants to break down the door of the fresh tomb. As they opened it, a sudden gust of wind blew out the lanterns, leaving them in the dark. Moments later, vivid white lightning flashed across the sky. Thunder boomed and roared above their heads. Six servants shivered in terror; the two youngest ran off into the dark.

"Get inside! Get inside!" Screaming and flailing at them with her wet silk scarf, Madame Peng herded the remaining servants into the tomb. Once inside, Housekeeper Ting lit a candle and then led the way toward Fong's coffin.

"Open it!" ordered Madame Peng shrilly.

As the servants began to pry the heavy cover off Fong's coffin, a terrible smell filled the tomb.

"Close it! Close it!" Madame Peng covered her nose with her handkerchief.

Housekeeper Ting held the candle above the coffin while other servants nailed it shut again.

"What's on the floor?" squealed Madame Peng. Leftover scraps of food were lying around Fong's coffin. The piece of jade that Madame Peng had placed in Fong's mouth was among the scraps, broken in half. Beside the jade was a piece of white silk with black writing on it. Housekeeper Ting shakily picked up the silken message and handed it to Madame Peng.

"'I'm hungry!'" Madame Peng read.

Screaming in fear, the servants dropped their tools and ran from the tomb into the dark night.

"Traitors! Come back here! You must obey me!" Madame Peng howled after them. Thunder and driving rain drowned out her words. She pounded her fists against the tomb. "Come back! You m-m-must obey me," she moaned, sobbing uncontrollably.

Madame Peng staggered back to the house and collapsed inside the red door. When she awoke, she found herself alone in the banquet hall. All the candles had gone out. By the lightning that flashed through the windows, Madame Peng found a matchbox and a lantern. Her shaking fingers managed to light it.

Calmed by the steady, warm glow of the light, Madame Peng felt some of her strength return.

"Those pathetic fools may have been afraid of you, Fong. I am not, for I know you. You are just a wicked girl. A dead wicked girl."

Madame Peng's stomach reminded her that she had not eaten since lunch. She walked to the servants' quarters next to the banquet hall.

Finding no one there, she went on to the kitchen. She dug through the pantries, but could find no food. "Wicked girl, it's not enough to humiliate me. You have to steal all my food, too!"

Finally she found a small bag of raw rice down in the cellar. She carried it to the kitchen.

"It has been years since I last cooked. But I still remember how to make fried rice. Let's see . . ." Madame Peng murmured as she poured water into a small pot and set it to boil on the kitchen fire. Once it was bubbling, she carefully added a few handfuls of rice.

She lit another lantern and went into the vegetable garden, walking carefully on the wet, slippery ground. The rain had stopped, and the earthy smell of the cool air revived her. There she found a garlic bulb and a few scallions. She walked to the henhouse and gathered a couple of fresh eggs.

By the time she returned to the kitchen, another storm front whipped the trees and spat rain against the windows. She lit an extra candle.

"Not much of a meal. But I will make the best of it." Madame Peng minced some garlic and scallions. She beat the eggs and scallions, adding a pinch of salt and pepper. She took the rice off the fire, then heated a little oil in a wok and dropped in the chopped garlic.

In a few moments, the delicious aroma of frying garlic stirred her hunger. She added the egg mixture and scrambled it. Now the most tantalizing smell Madame Peng could ever remember rose from the wok. For a moment her hunger left her weak.

She steadied herself, then turned to the pot of rice. "A humble meal, but right now it is a feast for a queen."

When she lifted the lid, she cried out in horror. The rice pot was empty!

She turned back to the wok. It, too, was empty!

Madame Peng fell to the floor, sobbing. "Thief! Show yourself!"

No one answered.

"Is it you, Fong? I am not afraid of your ghost," yelled Madame Peng. "Watch me! I am going to cook more food!"

Clutching the bag that held the last of the rice, Madame Peng stumbled out of the kitchen and into the garden. As she staggered toward the henhouse, the wind and rain beat on her mercilessly.

She hurried. Something caught her ankle and she tripped, falling hard. The bag flew from her hands, spraying rice across the mud.

Weeping, exhausted, and muddy, Madame Peng struggled

to sit up. She reached for the rice bag and tried to scoop up the scattered grains.

When she looked up, the small figure of a girl stood in front of the henhouse, dressed in silk the color of moonlight. Her eyes pierced the storm with flames of hatred. As she bent down to pick up an empty bowl, her long wet hair, dark as ink, draped across her face.

"Why don't you go back to your tomb, you ungrateful girl. I gave you the honor of dying with your father!" cried Madame Peng.

The reply came like a moan. "I want . . . FOOD . . . HUNGRY!"

Madame Peng screamed in terror, crawling desperately through the thick mud back to her house.

Several days passed before anyone came by the Yue house. Housekeeper Ting found the immaculate body of Madame Peng in her bed, dressed in pale white silk. Her hair was combed and perfumed. A jade bit protruded from her lips.

Even today, locals claim they have seen a figure dressed in silk the color of moonlight wandering through the village on stormy nights. So every fall, the villages there still hang bright lanterns around their houses and set out stir-fried rice on their porches to keep her away.

HUMAN SACRIFICES

Human sacrifice is recorded in China's earliest writings, dating back as far as the Shang dynasty, four thousand years ago. It was finally abolished in the early Ming dynasty, about C.E. 1500. During that time, when wealthy and powerful aristocrats died, some arranged for the sacrifice of their servants and close relatives to accompany them into the afterlife, so they could continue to enjoy their lavish lifestyle in death.

National Geographic News recently reported that Chinese archaeologists had excavated a 2,500-year-old tomb located in eastern China's Jiangxi Province. The tomb contained nearly four dozen victims of human sacrifice. In the past decade, archaeologists in Xi'an Province in northwest China discovered an ancient site containing more than six hundred tombs of those buried alive with their emperor, Shi Huangdi (221–210 B.C.E.), who started the ritual of building chambers for the sacrificed next to the owner of the tomb.

As a child, I had heard many terrifying stories about this ancient ritual. During my last trip to China, I visited two burial sites along the Yangtze River where this cruel custom was practiced—my inspiration for this story.

EGG STIR-FRIED RICE

You can be creative with this recipe. Feel free to replace the vegetables with others of your liking, or even with fresh fruit. Make sure the oil is hot enough before pouring in the eggs, so they will be fluffy. Let the cooked rice cool before stir-frying, to prevent it from sticking to the pan.

Makes 6 servings.

3 eggs

2 scallions, minced

2 teaspoons soy sauce

3 tablespoons canola oil

3 cloves garlic, chopped

1½ cups frozen green soybeans or peas

1 medium yellow bell pepper, seeded and chopped into 2-inch cubes

3 cups cooked rice

3 tablespoons soy sauce

2 teaspoons sesame oil

3 tablespoons dried cranberries or raisins

▓ Beat the eggs, scallions, and 2 teaspoons of soy sauce in a medium bowl. Heat 2 tablespoons canola oil in a pan over medium-high heat; swirl to coat pan. Add the egg mixture;

swirl to evenly cover the bottom of the pan. Cook, without stirring, for 30–40 seconds or until eggs are firm and brown on the bottom. Turn eggs and brown the other side. Chop eggs into small pieces with the spatula. Remove mixture from pan.

▦ Heat remaining 1 tablespoon canola oil in the same pan. Add garlic; stir-fry until fragrant, about 30 seconds. Add soybeans, stirring constantly for 1 minute. Add yellow pepper, stirring for another minute. Mix in the rice and the remaining 3 tablespoons of soy sauce, stirring constantly, until rice is heated through. Return the egg mixture to the pan; mix well. Garnish with sesame oil and dried cranberries. Serve hot.

DESSERTS

Jasmine Almond Cookies

OUTSIDE NEW YORK CITY there is a graveyard where many Chinatown residents bury their dead. On weekends, families often visit their loved ones' graves so they won't be forgotten.

The Lee family owned a Chinese restaurant, the Hollow Legs, situated in the very heart of Chinatown. The family had three boys, who were each born a year apart. The Lees named them after the restaurant's specialties: Drumsticks in Curry Sauce was the youngest, then Barbecue Ribs, and the oldest was Almond Cookie.

Two days before his thirteenth birthday, Almond Cookie died. He'd had a fight with his father and, in a blind rage, ran into the street without looking, only to be hit by a truck. The family had made it a tradition to go to his grave every week since his death, bringing with them his favorite dishes from the restaurant. Afterwards they stopped at the picnic shelter beside the graveyard, had lunch, and visited with friends.

Nearly a year after Almond Cookie's death, on April 4, Tomb Sweeping Day, the family went to the graveyard. As usual, Ribs carried a big basket of specialties from the Hollow Legs. Drumsticks carried a white trash bag and a little brush made of bamboo leaves.

From behind, even their parents had trouble telling them apart. Both boys had their father's wide shoulders and strong build. From the front, though, they were quite different. Drumsticks had many freckles, as if someone had spilled a cup of sesame seeds over him. Ribs had none. Drumsticks was full of questions and Ribs was always quick to answer his brother.

Carrying bundles of candles and incense, Mr. Lee marched like an army officer behind his sons. In fact, he had served in Taiwan's Republic of China Army before he opened his small restaurant in Chinatown.

Mrs. Lee was as slender as a willow. Her buckteeth made her lips protrude slightly on her smooth face. Carrying a big stack of paper funeral money, she panted, struggling to keep up. Her forehead was damp with sweat despite the cool autumn breeze.

When they came within sight of Almond Cookie's grave, Drumsticks ran ahead. His job was to clean up the grave site, so the family could set up fresh food and burn the funeral money as offerings.

"All the food from last week is gone!" yelled Drumsticks. "Who ate it?"

"Almond Cookie! He must have been hungry," replied Ribs. "Oh, look! There's something on his tombstone." He lifted a small rock off a piece of scorched funeral money with something written on it.

Mr. Lee walked up. "What's this?" he asked.

Ribs read aloud, "Mu shu chicken, crispy duck, chicken nest, pepper steak, tea-smoked salmon, shrimp chow mein, green-tea ice cream, jasmine almond cookies . . ." It was a list of the restaurant's special dishes.

"He's placing an order!" Drumsticks exclaimed.

Mrs. Lee fell to her knees. "Oh dear! My poor boy! He's hungry."

"He wrote it?" Drumsticks peered over Ribs's shoulder. "I remember his handwriting was hard to read."

"Of course he did." Ribs handed the note to Mr. Lee. "Maybe his penmanship improved in heaven."

"How do you know?" Drumsticks asked skeptically.

"His ghost has come out for the festival," interrupted Mrs. Lee. "No wonder I dreamed about him last night." Tears rolled down her face.

"Why doesn't he come out when we're here? Would he—"

"Don't ever say that," Mr. Lee interrupted, raising his

voice sharply. "Some ghosts are angry spirits. It's best that they stay in their own world."

Mrs. Lee stroked the tombstone and wept. "Almond Cookie, don't save money. If you're hungry, use the money to buy food in heaven."

"Maybe he has trouble finding food he likes," said Drumsticks. "Remember how picky he was?"

"Almond Cookie, let us know what you want," Mrs. Lee continued. "We will bring it to you."

Drumsticks looked at the list. "But how did Almond Cookie know to ask for our new specialty, jasmine almond cookies? We didn't put jasmine in the cookies when he was alive."

"Well, ghosts know things," Ribs said as he grabbed the list from Drumsticks.

"We can't let him be a hungry ghost. We'll bring him more food next week," said Mr. Lee. He set part of the family's lunch, a large lotus leaf stuffed with sweet rice, and a few roasted pork dumplings, next to the dishes Ribs and Drumsticks had already set out. "Hopefully these will keep him fed for a while."

Mrs. Lee lit a bundle of incense. The smell of jasmine filled the air. "My dear Almond Cookie, see the smoke from the incense? We are thinking about you every day." She sobbed.

Drumsticks piled stacks of funeral money in front of the grave and lit them with a cigarette lighter. The family waited until the money burned down to black ashes before setting out for the picnic shelter.

"Hello, hello," Mr. Lee called out to Mrs. Qian and Mr. Zong, who were sitting beside each other at one end of the picnic table. They were longtime customers and family friends.

Mr. Zong had previously owned a jewelry store, and Mrs. Qian ran a hair salon. Both had recently lost their spouses. They often played mahjong together after dinner, unless Mrs. Qian was helping out at the restaurant when the Lees took time off.

"Please come join us for lunch." Mrs. Qian moved her jacket from the table to her lap to make room for the Lees. Her smile wrinkled her face like a blossoming chrysanthemum.

Ribs and Drumsticks privately referred to her as "Mrs. Chicken Nest," because her frizzy perm resembled a popular crispy noodle dish served in the restaurant. Mrs. Qian's husband had died from cancer three years ago.

"Yes, yes, come and sit." Mr. Zong waved them to the table. He was a small man with a graying mustache above his thin lips. He had served with Mr. Lee in the army. Even though he was an old family friend, Ribs and Drumsticks disliked him. When he wasn't smoking, he was chewing on one thing or another, often sunflower seeds. He had an annoying habit of spitting the shells all around him, regardless of whose shoes or bags were in the way.

They also thought he was strange, wearing his wife's jade bracelet ever since she died the year before. She had hanged herself in the middle of their jewelry store the morning the bank foreclosed on it. Now Mr. Zong worked as a clerk in a different jewelry store down the block from the restaurant.

Mr. and Mrs. Lee sat across from their friends and the two boys sat beside their parents. Mrs. Lee spread out what remained of their lunch: a take-out box of rice, three spring rolls, and two sesame balls. Mr. Lee poured hot tea from a Thermos into paper cups and passed them out to everyone.

"The strangest thing happened today." With tears in her eyes, Mrs. Lee told their friends about the note.

"Oh my, that is strange!" exclaimed Mrs. Qian. "Nothing like that has ever happened at my husband's grave. Now your poor boys don't have enough for lunch. I have some extra steamed buns. Here." Mrs. Qian shifted her heavy frame and pushed a bowl in front of Drumsticks and Ribs.

The boys looked uncertainly at each other. Were they hungry enough to dare eat one of her buns? Mrs. Qian was renowned for her bad cooking. Their father once joked that it was a good thing Mrs. Qian ran a hair salon rather than a restaurant.

"Nothing like that has ever happened at my wife's grave either. I do miss her food," Mr. Zong said sorrowfully. He often told the Lees that their restaurant's cooking was the only close match to his wife's.

Mrs. Lee broke a spring roll in half and shared it with Mr. Lee. The adults continued their conversation about the hungry ghost. The boys stopped chewing when Mrs. Qian said in her high-pitched voice that hungry ghosts were the angriest kind. "They are capable of anything!"

Mr. Zong set down his teacup and said, "No one has ever really seen a ghost. But to be safe, just bring Almond Cookie more food." He took a steamed bun from the bowl for himself and pushed it in front of Ribs. "Here! Have a bun!"

Catching a sideways glance from his mother, Ribs rubbed his half-empty tummy. "*Bǎo-le, bǎo-le*—Too full, too full!" he politely refused.

After Almond Cookie died, Ribs had inherited the job of delivering Mr. Zong's take-out orders. Back when Almond Cookie was alive and Mr. Zong had his store, he often ordered five-course meals. These days he ordered only the cheapest dishes on the menu—stir-fried rice or noodles.

Ribs angrily recalled an incident the previous week. That Friday, Mr. Zong had splurged and ordered the shrimp chow mein. When Ribs arrived at the jewelry shop, Mr. Zong insisted that Ribs wait there until he had spread the noodles out on a big plate and counted the shrimp. Other clerks and the customers gathered around to watch the scene with amusement.

"There should be a dozen! I only have eleven here," he had exclaimed. "I refuse to pay the delivery fee!"

Ribs knew better than to argue. Mr. Zong would surely call up his father to complain, like the time Mr. Zong complained about Almond Cookie's bad attitude and lack of respect for his elders.

A few days after their visit to the cemetery, Drumsticks and Ribs came home from school and found their parents packing food into baskets.

"We're going to the graveyard," said Mrs. Lee glumly.

"What about the restaurant?" Ribs asked.

"Mrs. Qian offered to take over for today. I can't let Almond Cookie wait until the weekend." Mrs. Lee stuffed one more bag of fortune cookies into the basket. With everybody's hands filled with baskets and bags, the family headed out.

At Almond Cookie's grave, they found all the food gone and another stone anchoring a note written on a piece of funeral money.

As Drumsticks read it, everyone's eyes widened.

"Mu shu chicken—overcooked; crispy duck—too salty . . ."

". . . chicken nest—noodles not crunchy," Ribs continued. "Pepper steak—just right, but not enough."

Mrs. Lee fell to the ground. "Papa, I told you to cook a double batch of pepper steak." She wept.

Mr. Lee grabbed the note and quickly read the rest of it. "-Tea-smoked salmon—too much tea . . . almond cookies—not sweet enough . . . green-tea ice cream—melted. Next time bring sweet red bean dumplings. Shrimp chow mein—only eleven shrimp."

Mrs. Lee burst out crying. "He's come back to haunt us. If we can't make him happy, something bad will happen."

Without burning funeral money or lighting candles, the family set out the food and left.

That night, Mr. and Mrs. Lee didn't eat dinner and went to bed early.

"We should go to the graveyard tonight," Ribs whispered to Drumsticks as they absentmindedly picked at some leftover noodles.

Drumsticks quickly drew a sharp breath. "Why?"

"Because Mr. Zong is stealing Almond Cookie's food," said Ribs. "Think about the note. Almond Cookie was a picky eater, but never that finicky. Mr. Zong is the only one I know who counts the shrimp."

Wide-eyed, Drumsticks nodded. "He'll know that we took food to Almond Cookie's grave today because Mrs. Qian is at the restaurant and won't be playing mahjong."

Ribs stabbed at the noodles with his chopsticks. "Don't tell Mom and Dad. They won't believe us," he said with a groan.

"Just like the time Mr. Zong complained about Almond Cookie," Ribs said gloomily. "And Dad took Mr. Zong's side."

"If not for his complaint, Almond Cookie would still be alive." Drumsticks slapped his chopsticks down on the table.

Ribs stood up. "Let's disguise ourselves in our Halloween skeleton costumes. And bring our baseball bats, just in case."

"Yeah!" Drumsticks grinned.

The boys quietly slipped out of the house, carrying their baseball bats over their shoulders and their costumes in takeout bags from the Hollow Legs. They took the subway to the last stop outside the city.

A silver bank of clouds scudded across the full moon that illuminated the quiet street. Ribs and Drumsticks walked toward the cemetery with their shadows ominously trailing behind them. Bats flew through the shadows, hunting for a midnight dinner. The brothers shivered in the warm spring breeze.

As they passed the picnic shelter, Drumsticks asked in a small voice, "Are you sure it is Mr. Zong? What if he doesn't come tonight?"

"It's him," Ribs said confidently. "He's gonna be here. Shhhh," he whispered. "I can smell barbecued ribs. Look! The food's still here." He pointed to a grave on the right side of the narrow path.

Drumsticks hugged himself, shivering. "Do you think any ghosts will come out?"

Ribs crouched down behind the tombstone across from Almond Cookie's grave and took the skeleton costumes out of the bags. "If they do, they won't hurt us when they see us in these costumes."

"What time is it?" Drumsticks asked as he tied up the back of Ribs's costume. "I read that ghosts come out at midnight."

Ribs glanced at his watch. "Ten to midnight." He slid on his gloves while Drumsticks pulled on his mask. Owls hooted in the nearby trees. The boys nervously peered about the surrounding tombstones and bushes.

Ribs tugged on Drumsticks's sleeve and pointed in the direction they'd just come. A black shadow moved slowly between the graves.

"So-ome-one is co-oming?" Drumsticks's teeth chattered. He gripped his baseball bat in a death choke.

"H-e's c-coming toward u-us." Ribs pulled Drumsticks closer.

The figure stopped in front of Almond Cookie's grave. The boys held their breath and peeked out from behind the tombstone. The figure took out a pair of chopsticks and opened a big bag. Removing a stack of boxes, it transferred food from the bowls into the containers until it reached the crispy duck. The dark figure paused, put down the chopsticks, and lifted a duck leg to its mouth. It took a huge bite, smacking its lips in delight. Then its black hood fell back, revealing a face in the bright moonlight.

Drumsticks and Ribs jumped out and raced toward Mr. Zong. "It's you! Thief!" they yelled, waving their baseball bats.

"Get lost!" Ribs shoved Mr. Zong away from the food. Mr. Zong stumbled and fell on Almond Cookie's grave.

Abruptly, the ground shook, dirt rushed up, and the grave cracked open. A white skeletal hand shot out, grabbing Mr. Zong's ankle. Half of his leg disappeared into the grave.

"Help me!" cried Mr. Zong. He waved his hands and kicked with his free leg, scattering food and dirt all around.

Ribs and Drumsticks snapped out of their shock, dropped their baseball bats, and grabbed Mr. Zong's arms.

"Ahh, please, please help me!" screamed Mr. Zong. His hands groped and grasped at the boys. Cold sweat rolled down Ribs's and Drumsticks's backs. They pulled at Mr. Zong's arms as hard as they could, until Drumsticks slipped and lost his grip.

Another bony hand reached out to grab Mr. Zong's other leg. Mr. Zong was pulled down into the ground, his free hand clawing at the dirt. Frantic, he clutched Ribs's arm with both hands, dragging Ribs down to his knees. Ribs cried out in panic, punching at Mr. Zong's arms. Drumsticks tried in vain to break Mr. Zong's grip on Ribs.

Suddenly, a low laugh came from below, followed by the horrifying sound of cracking bones and chewing.

Mr. Zong screamed like an injured animal. He let go of Ribs and sank into the crack, his cries smothered as earth sealed over him.

Ribs and Drumsticks fell onto the ground, shaking in fear. They vowed never to tell a living soul about that night because no one would ever believe them.

Weeks later, after an extensive investigation, the police found only a single clue in the case of Mr. Zong's disappearance—a broken jade bracelet in the graveyard outside New York City, resting upon Almond Cookie's grave.

TOMB SWEEPING DAY AND CHINESE ARMIES

Qīng Míng (Tomb Sweeping Day), which means "Clear Brightness," is one of the few traditional Chinese holidays that follow the solar calendar, typically falling around April 4.

The holiday is a time for the living to pay their respects to the deceased and to care for their graves. The family lights incense and candles. Money, jewelry, clothing, furniture, and other necessities—all in the form of paper—are burned as offerings. It's believed the money and gifts ensure the deceased have a comfortable afterlife in heaven.

Food acts as a bridge between the living and the dead. Families offer elaborate dishes to their loved ones at the graves so they don't go hungry and beg for food from other ghosts. Usually, the family pays more frequent visits to the newly deceased, especially around the time of Tomb Sweeping Day. In return, the happy spirits of the dead look after family members and ensure them a bountiful, safe year.

Every year since my parents passed away, my brothers in China call to tell me about the trips they have made to the graves of my grandparents and parents on Tomb Sweeping Day. They let me know in detail the food they brought and the items they burned in front of their graves. When possible, I plan trips back to China in early April so I can go to the graveyard to pay my respects.

The Republic of China Army began as the National Revolutionary Army in 1924. It fought against the Communists during the Chinese Communist Revolution of the 1940s. When the People's Liberation Army won the revolution, the remnants of the National Revolutionary Army retreated to Taiwan along with the government. It was later reformed into the Republic of China Army.

Since 1949, the ROC Army and the PLA have stood in opposition of each other across the narrow straits of the China Sea that separate the People's Republic of China and Taiwan.

JASMINE ALMOND COOKIES

These tasty cookies are easy to make and will last up to a week if stored in an airtight container. The fresh aroma of jasmine will give the cookies a delicate flavor. Enjoy them with a cup of tea and a scoop of your favorite ice cream.

Makes 40 cookies.

¼ cup plus 2 tablespoons butter at room temperature

¼ cup almond butter

½ cup plus 2 tablespoons sugar

1 egg, lightly beaten

½ teaspoon almond extract

¾ cup all-purpose flour

contents of 3 jasmine green tea bags

½ teaspoon baking soda

⅛ teaspoon salt

40 unblanched whole almonds

▥ Preheat oven to 350°F (about 175°C). In a large bowl, combine butter, almond butter, and sugar. Place in oven for 3 to 5 minutes, until butter starts to soften. Mix until light and fluffy; beat in egg and almond extract.

◾ Add the flour, tea, baking soda, and salt to egg mixture and beat until combined.

◾ Spray a ½-tablespoon measuring spoon with nonstick cooking spray. Spoon balls of dough onto lightly greased baking sheets, about 2 inches apart. Press an almond into the center of each ball.

◾ Bake 12 to 14 minutes or until cookies are lightly brown. Let cookies cool completely on baking sheets. Store in an airtight container.

Eight-Treasure
Rice Pudding

I N 1992, A GROUP OF FARMERS digging a well in northern China uncovered a flooded underground passage. The government brought in a team of archaeologists to investigate. They discovered two stone lions, guardians against demons, standing at the mouth of a corridor that led to a pair of chambers. Each chamber contained one white marble coffin laid atop an alabaster platform. The remains of a man in his fifties occupied the left coffin, where a pleasant tea aroma lingered. The remains of a boy in his teens resided in the right one. Judging from the luxurious items inside the chambers, such as bronze and gold artifacts, elaborate silk gowns, and ornately carved redwood furniture, the occupants had been members of a wealthy family.

The bodies were so well preserved that their skin and

muscles were still pliant. The similarities in their facial features—flat nose, droopy lips, and the angular shape of their skulls—suggested that they were related, probably father and son.

What startled the archaeologists were the anguished expressions of the two. They suspected that both had died in excruciating pain. Some unusual artifacts further aroused the interest of the archaeologists. Twenty bamboo baskets filled with high-quality West Lake Dragon Well tea surrounded the father. In his folded hands rested a dark red teacup engraved with the yin-yang symbol, denoting harmonious balance.

Around the boy's coffin rested five small earthen jars, each containing the corpse of a praying mantis. Across his breast, his right hand clasped a pair of silver chopsticks. Surprisingly, though the tips were blackened, the rest of the chopsticks hadn't tarnished over time.

Further investigation determined, from trace amounts found in his digestive tract, that the father had died from poisoning. However, the boy's cause of death remained unexplained.

"Go to fight!"

Wei ran the dry tip of his thick camel-hair calligraphy brush down the back of his new mantis. His old tutor's head paused mid-bob, glancing up. His mouth hung half open for a moment before he closed his eyes again and resumed his recitation of a long, rambling poem:

Rabbit falls into the dog hole,
Cat hides behind the grain.
I'll boil the grain and make rice,
I'll pluck the carrots and make soup.
Rice and carrots are both cooked,
Should I invite Rabbit
Or Cat to eat with me?

Wei had released his mantises from their earthen jars to stave off the mind-numbing boredom of his tutor's lesson. For all he cared, the cat could eat both the soup and the rabbit.

The new mantis turned and energetically boxed with the tip of Wei's brush. His first mantis stood beside it, as still as the brown twig it resembled. Sunlight filtered in through the window and the open doorway, casting the two mantises in a golden glow. Wei's heart filled with pride as he observed the new green mantis aggressively attacking his brush.

"I'll have to feed these little fighters soon," Wei murmured. His mantises required a prodigious number of crickets every day to stay fit. Fortunately, the kids in town were willing to collect crickets for a few coins. He envied them, not having to bear the burden of these foolish lessons.

All morning, Wei hardly registered the meandering lecture his tutor gave about the poem's author and its deep connotations. The tutor was either too lost in his own thoughts to notice Wei's lack of attention, or had resigned himself to it.

Since his early youth, Wei had been fascinated by the mantis battles staged in grimy alleys or behind shabby tea halls. Without a mother to watch over him, and his father's hands full running his tea company, Wei had little supervision. He took full advantage of his freedom, roaming the streets for mantis fights and enjoying the excitement of the crowds.

However, last year, when Wei turned fifteen, his father, Master Shi, finally noticed this thin, angular boy in his home, now almost as tall as himself. Realizing the importance of educating his only son to carry on the family name, he set forth ludicrous rules, demanding that Wei study diligently for long hours to prepare for the imperial exam.

Wei had to rise with the sun each day to read literature and recite poems until bedtime. He was also banned from attending mantis fights, though this didn't stop him. He began to host small fights in his garden in the morning, when his father attended to the tea shop. So far, none of the servants had informed his father about his indiscretions—they all knew Wei would eventually become their master.

Master Shi had hired the old tutor because the man was renowned for his ability to foresee the questions on the competitive and unpredictable imperial exam. Master Shi wanted Wei to become an important court official. "Our Shi family has no lack of money," he often declared. "Power is what we need next!"

Despite his father's urgings, Wei didn't aspire to become a

minor bureaucrat, forever condemned to kowtow to higher-ups. His dream was to own the most powerful mantis in town and earn the respect of his friends and fellow mantis fighters.

Emboldened by Master Shi's ignorance, each day Wei took audacious risks to break his father's rules. Recently he had purchased this new mantis, bigger, stronger, and more aggressive than any he had ever owned.

Shifting the tip of his brush, Wei smiled with admiration as his green mantis followed it closely with its large eyes. The mantis was absolutely magnificent, a compact fighting machine. It was worth every silver coin it had cost, even though it had almost exhausted his savings. With this mantis he was confident he would win back all that money in no time.

Wei focused on encouraging his mantises to fight, until he caught the aroma of West Lake Dragon Well tea. Wei's heart thundered as he quickly made a tent out of his book to cover both mantises. His father was coming! A silhouette filled the doorway.

Abruptly, the tutor jerked to full wakefulness and rose to his feet with lightning speed. He bowed obsequiously, his long white beard dusting the table in front of him. "*Ni hao*—Hello, Master Shi!"

Master Shi did not look like a typical tea merchant. He was tall and powerfully built. The square hat he wore accentuated his resemblance to a general of the imperial army and declared his lofty social status. He grunted dismissively at the tutor and turned to Wei.

"How are your studies progressing?" he inquired. His bushy silver mustache quivered.

"Fine," Wei answered nervously, glancing quickly down at the book. The green mantis poked out its head.

Master Shi followed his gaze and plucked up the book, revealing the two mantises.

"Is this what you are teaching him?" he demanded, glaring at the tutor.

The tutor's eyes grew wide and his complexion paled. "Ah, ah . . ."

The green mantis held its forearms up like two clubs and shuffled to the left. It parried a strike from the brown mantis and jabbed an arm straight out. Their forearms interlocked and the two wrestled briefly.

Master Shi appeared to exude the essence of calm as he closed the book. Wei would have known better, had he not been staring at his mantises, regretting that he had let them out.

Whack! Blinding pain swept across Wei's face! *Whack! Whack!*

Wei screamed and clutched his forehead with his hands. Something warm ran down his nose. Drops of blood stained his yellow silk robe.

Master Shi spun and pointed at the tutor. "Go!" he shouted. "You useless old fool."

Stumbling into the courtyard, the tutor paused outside the door and yelled, "I did my best! You can't make a tiger from turtle droppings!"

"Incompetent old fool! You couldn't teach a turtle to crawl!" barked Master Shi.

Master Shi turned to face Wei. "Lazy boy! Spoiled and stupid! I will hire Tutor Xu, the strictest teacher in all of Suzhou, to set you straight." He looked down at the mantises. The green one had ripped off one of the brown one's legs and was in the process of removing another.

"And you will stop wasting your time on these stupid bugs." He raised up the book and slammed it on the two mantises. Wei's stomach churned and he froze with impotent rage. His hands curled into claws under the table.

Moments after Master Shi swept from the room, Wei let out a whimper of dismay. His mantises! He lifted up the book. Their heads were detached, and arms and legs were scattered. Guts from their burst abdomens stained the cover. He sat there weeping until the sun faded and the room grew dark. Finally, the waves of anger receded as he formed a plot against his father.

That night, he waited until the entire household was asleep. With a small black lantern in hand, he snuck into the warehouse located behind the garden. After groping in

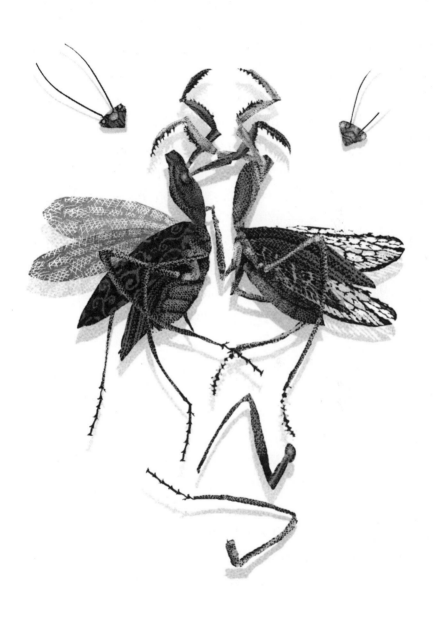

the dim light for a long moment, he found the closet door he sought behind a basket of tea leaves. From there he took a dark red wooden box from the top shelf. It held a special white powder meant for the rats.

The next morning, Wei appeared in the kitchen as the cook, a man with a full shock of white hair and broad shoulders, prepared breakfast. On the table in the center of the room, a dark red engraved tray held a white porcelain pot with matching bowls and spoons.

The delicate steamy aroma from the pot told Wei that it held his father's habitual breakfast—chicken congee.

"I will serve this to my father," said Wei, taking the tray. The cook shrugged and turned back to place a few buns inside a steamer.

Once in the hallway, Wei quickly set the tray on a nearby redwood bench. Glancing around to make sure no one was in sight, he took a pair of silver chopsticks and a small paper packet from his left sleeve. He opened the packet and shook the powder into the congee then mixed it in briskly with the chopsticks. When he removed the chopsticks, he was surprised to see that their tips had turned black. He wiped them off on the side of his robe and hid them again in his wide sleeve.

When Wei entered the dining room with the tray, his father sat imposingly at the head of the table. He chatted amiably with his new concubine beside him who had a face painted like the teahouse opera singers. Master Shi stopped talking and glared at Wei.

"Father, please forgive my previous transgressions. I promise I will do better in the future." Wei set the tray next to his father's teacup and the pot of Dragon Well tea. The tea set had been fired from the finest dark red clay, with a yin-yang symbol carved in relief on the sides. Wei bowed low. "Father, may I serve your congee?" he asked solemnly.

Master Shi's eyebrows rose in surprise, and then relaxed. He nodded slightly in approval.

"I am glad to see that you have finally come to your senses."

"Yes, Father." With one of the porcelain spoons, Wei scooped congee from the pot into a bowl. *Pompous old man! So full of himself*, thought Wei, working to keep his face meek.

"Good! If you apply yourself to your studies the way you did to those useless bugs, I am sure you will do well in government. And once you are in, I won't have to bribe all those petty officials anymore."

Wei almost lost control when his father mentioned his beloved mantises. Taking a slow breath, he inverted the spoon and laid the handle across the lip of the bowl, then carefully set it before his father.

"Would you like some, too, Third Mother?" Wei asked respectfully.

"No, it's too plain for my taste," she replied coolly.

Too bad, thought Wei.

"Why do you eat such bland foods, Master?" asked the concubine in her wheedling voice.

"When you work with tea, you have to be scrupulous about what you eat," said Master Shi. "Soon you will learn all the rules of this household."

The smile on the concubine's face faded.

Wei remembered the beatings he'd received when he bought food from street vendors. The last time, when he was caught enjoying a bowl of noodles in spicy sesame sauce, his father hit him so hard it had taken weeks for the bruises to fade.

Master Shi continued, "Dragon Well tea is the finest in China. It's famous for its pure and delicate flavor." He paused to slurp down some congee.

"This superb tea will be ruined if it absorbs any odors. That is why I ban any strongly flavored foods from our household: peppers, nuts, smoked meats, and preserved vegetables—none of that! Imagine my tea tasting like kung pao shrimp!"

He coughed loudly and patted his chest. After clearing his throat, Master Shi slurped some more congee, nearly emptying the bowl. "Congee and mild steamed foods are ideal." He set down the spoon and lifted his teacup. "If the tea is to pick up any odor from me, it will be its own!" He looked at Wei and smiled proudly. "Remember what I just said. Even though you will become a government official after you pass your exam, our family fortune and reputation rests on the quality of our tea."

Master Shi took a sip, grimacing at a disturbance in his stomach.

Frowning abruptly, he set down the cup. "Ohhh," he moaned softly. Sweat broke out across his broad forehead. He hugged his stomach. "I have to go . . ." He rose and strode out of the room.

The concubine followed. Master Shi's loud cries of pain came from the hallway, accompanied by the concubine's shrill screams. Wei stared at the table with a slight smile. No one would ever hurt his mantises again.

It took all of five hours for Master Shi to die. Wei stood nearby, trying to act like a worried and dutiful son, even managing a few tears now and then. The entire time Master Shi was in terrible agony, suffering from intense stomach cramps, explosive diarrhea, and rampant vomiting. Luckily, Master Shi's physician misdiagnosed his illness as cholera.

Wei had nothing to worry about. He was free!

Now the new Master Shi, Wei took great pleasure in kicking the two concubines out of the house right after the funeral. To his delight, his father's servants and employees now took orders from him, unquestioningly.

After three grueling days of trying to run his father's tea company, Wei gave up. He went out and spent a small fortune on five powerful mantises. Back home, he lifted the ban on strongly flavored foods. He was ready to enjoy life—good food and formidable mantises. He invited his best friends over for a mantis competition.

"Go, go! Jump, my boy!" yelled Wei to his newest mantis. It had been winning on the battleground all afternoon. Wei and his three friends surrounded a large round table littered with insect parts.

"Wei, you've got yourself a fierce mantis!" Ban laughed heartily, jutting out his pointed chin, his slim arm slapping his bony knee.

"*Ai yo!* It's tearing off the head of my mantis!" cried Cai, his flushed, pimply face contrasting harshly with his green silken robe, decorated with a tiger.

"What did you expect?" snapped Wei. "You get what you pay for. Mine cost five times more than your little donkey." He snickered, displaying his tea-stained teeth.

Liang, the shortest among them, raised his hands in a placating gesture. "Please, it is the insects that should fight, not us. Besides, the food has arrived!" He rolled up the sleeves of his red silk robe, embroidered with a dragon.

Two servants entered cautiously. One carried a large bowl of spicy beef noodles, the other bore a bottle of rice wine.

Wei carefully scooped his beloved mantis into its jar. Before shutting the lid, he dropped in a few crickets. Content that his precious pet also had its meal, he placed the jar on a small table next to him.

The servants quietly cleaned up the dismembered insects, poured wine into big cups, and divided the noodles among the bowls.

As Wei stirred a bowl of noodles with his silver chopsticks, the aroma of Dragon Well tea wafted across his face. Startled, he furtively looked around the room. When he found nothing alarming, he silently berated himself for his foolishness. He must have imagined the odor. Wei had watched the servants seal his father's tomb.

Wei was about to take a bite of the delectable noodles when he noticed his silver chopsticks—

"Ah!" he cried, tossing the chopsticks away.

His friends jerked their heads in his direction and stopped eating.

"My chopsticks . . ."

Ban, who was closest to him, swallowed and picked up the chopsticks. "What's wrong?"

"They bit him!" said Cai, laughing.

"They turned black!" exclaimed Wei.

"So what? Maybe they need to be polished," said Cai.

"No, they don't," said Ban, examining them. "They're fine. Here."

"NO!" Wei slapped Ban's hand. The chopsticks clattered on the floor. "Get out!" he yelled.

His friends didn't move, staring at him wide-eyed, not sure if he was joking or serious. Wei stood up abruptly and heaved bowls off the table, scattering slippery noodles everywhere.

"OUT! OUT!" he screamed.

His friends quickly stood and picked up their mantis jars. "Let's go."

"He's gone crazy!" they murmured as they stomped out.

Wei picked up his chopsticks. What had happened? They were untarnished. *Who just tried to poison me? I can trust no one! I can't accuse anyone either, not without giving myself away.*

Wei stalked off to the kitchen. There he found the cook grinding soybeans in a stone mortar.

"Those noodles you made for me today," he said. "Show me how you made them, every step."

The cook stared at Wei for a long moment, looking confused.

"Now!" barked Wei.

The cook composed himself quickly. "It is very easy, Master Shi. I would be honored to show you."

He kneaded flour, eggs, and water into dough. He skillfully stretched the dough into long, thin strands then added them to boiling water.

After draining the noodles, the cook sautéed ginger, garlic, and chili in a wok and tossed in some minced meat and bok choy. "Now I put in the noodles," said the cook, pouring them into the sizzling, snapping wok. He stirred the noodles around a bit and then mixed in a few spoons of soy sauce and garlic paste. He finished off by drizzling in a little sesame oil.

"Done!" he proclaimed, nodding happily. The cook hooked some noodles on his chopsticks and slurped them down.

"Delicious!" he exclaimed.

The gut-wrenching aroma brought tears to Wei's eyes. He hadn't realized how hungry he was. Eagerly, he took his chopsticks from his sleeve, stirred the noodles in the wok, and—caught the scent of Dragon Well tea. The tips of his chopsticks had turned black!

Heart pounding, Wei fought for self-control. How could this be? He'd watched the cook's every move. He'd even seen the cook taste the noodles!

Wei vigorously polished his chopsticks. He was convinced the cook had somehow tried to poison him.

Voice shaking, he barked, "It looks awful! You are fired."

That same day, Wei hired a new cook and followed him everywhere, even going with him to the market. Yet every time Wei's chopsticks touched the finished dish, the aroma of Dragon Well tea wafted around him and the tips turned black. He dismissed the second cook.

By the next day, his hunger had made him weak and dizzy. Wei stumbled around the city's market, desperate for something to eat. He paused before one open-air stall where a heavyset man busily fed branches into a brick stove, his round face sweating profusely in the heat.

"What are you cooking?" asked Wei in a weak voice.

"A traditional dessert, young master," replied the cook, turning to Wei. "Eight-treasure rice pudding." His mouth stretched into a broad smile.

"What's in it?" Wei lifted the lid off of the steam basket. A tantalizing cloud of steam rose up, permeating the air. Inside was a large ceramic bowl filled to the brim. Wei leaned over and took deep whiffs.

"Sweet rice, as you see. It also contains peanuts, honey, and dried fruits, such as raisins, cherries, mango . . ." The cook took the lid from Wei and placed it back on.

Wei had only heard about most of these ingredients. His anger toward his father resurfaced. How could the old fool have deprived him of such splendid foods?

The sweet scent aroused a pang in his stomach and made him even weaker; Wei leaned against the wall as he drooled uncontrollably. He decided that once he found a cook he could trust, he would have this dish made every day. He thought about the raisins, a rare treat his father considered "too pungent." He'd tasted them only once before. Now he imagined them growing plump in the steaming rice.

Wei threw a handful of silver coins into the wooden box on the counter. "Is it ready yet?" he asked eagerly.

"I think so, young master." The cheerful cook quickly lifted the lid and removed the eight-treasure rice pudding. He covered the bowl with a plate, quickly inverted the dishes, and rapped the plate on the counter. Carefully lifting the bowl, he revealed the jewel-like dessert, crowned with the colorful fruits, honey, and nuts. The cook nodded approvingly.

Wei eagerly waited with his chopsticks in hand. "Taste it! Hurry!" he ordered, handing his chopsticks to the cook.

The cook scooped up a bite of the rice mixture. "It's hot. Mmm, delicious!" he exclaimed, his eyes half closed.

"Have some more," ordered Wei. He watched the cook intently as he took more bites.

"It is cooked perfectly. The rice isn't too chewy or pasty, and there's just the right amount of honey." The cook waved the chopsticks in the air. "The nuts and dried fruit complement each other nicely . . ." he rambled on.

Wei grabbed his chopsticks from the cook and stirred the eight-treasure rice pudding, ruining its beautiful presentation. He struggled to contain his excitement.

For the first time in two days, he didn't smell Dragon Well tea. Most important, the chopsticks didn't turn black! Filled with excitement, he stuffed a large clump into his mouth. The rice was so moist, the raisins so succulent! The honey coated everything with a delectable sweetness, and the fruit and nuts burst with flavors. He had never tasted anything as delicious as this.

But something was wrong!

His tongue felt enormous, and he began to wheeze through swollen lips. Bumps roughened the inside of his mouth. Wei couldn't breathe through his nose anymore. His stomach hurt. Agh, it was burning agony!

Wei doubled over in pain, dropping his chopsticks. He groaned because he could no longer draw breath to scream. His vision tunneled, with only his silver chopsticks visible on the ground, next to his fingertips. Spasms racked his body. Wei released a final wheeze. His eyes bulged and his swollen lips twisted in a silent scream.

A rumor quickly spread that Wei had poisoned his father and that Master Shi's ghost had killed Wei, in a revenge strike from the grave.

A year after the tomb's discovery, a brilliant young forensic pathologist solved the mystery of the boy's death—anaphylactic shock, brought on by a severe allergy to peanuts. However, no one could explain why just the tips of the boy's chopsticks had turned black. Despite numerous tests, they couldn't detect a trace of arsenic or any other poison.

MANTIS FIGHTS, DRAGON WELL TEA, AND ARSENIC

Mantis fights were a very popular pastime in ancient China, much as American football is today. One of the emperors even had an entire village dedicated to breeding mantises for him. A good mantis was worth more than a pound of gold, and in some social circles a person's status was based on his mantis's prowess at combat.

As a child, I often attended my brothers' praying mantis fights with the other boys in our courtyard. I even joined their search for mantises in the field, but I was never brave enough to capture one, afraid the mantis would bite me.

West Lake Dragon Well tea is one of the best in China. Due to its delicate flavor, in ancient times, high-class tea merchants established strict rules and rituals for handling tea to preserve the subtle flavor. They forbade staff from consuming foods with strong flavors, such as garlic and nuts, or alcoholic drinks.

Arsenic was a popular poison to use as a murder weapon in ancient China. It eventually received the nickname of "Inheritance Powder," because impatient heirs would poison their benefactors to speed up their own rise to power. Arsenic reacts with silver, causing it to turn black, so many of the rich and powerful ate with silver chopsticks to prevent an untimely death.

Back then, people were unaware of food allergies. Therefore, when a person died from anaphylactic shock, others might blame it on poison, ghosts, curses, or witchcraft.